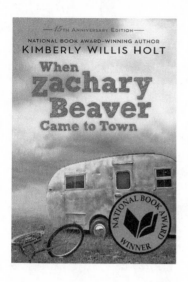

—15TH ANNIVERSARY EDITION—
NATIONAL BOOK AWARD–WINNING AUTHOR
KIMBERLY WILLIS HOLT

When
**zachary
Beaver**
Came to Town

NATIONAL BOOK AWARD WINNER

Travel back to the special place where it all began . . .

Winner of the National Book Award for Young People's Literature

An ALA Notable Book

One of ALA's Top Ten Best Books for Young Adults

The Horn Book Fanfare

A *School Library Journal* Best Book of the Year

"This book packs more emotional power than 90% of the so-called grown-up novels taking up precious space on bookshelves around the country."—*USA Today*

★ "Holt reinvents the coming-of-age story."
—*Kirkus Reviews*, starred review

★ "In her own down-to-earth, people-smart way, Holt offers a gift."—*The Horn Book*, starred review

★ "Holt humanizes the outsider without sentimentality . . . she reveals the freak in all of us, and the power of redemption."
—*Booklist*, starred review

★ "[Holt's] heartwarming and carefully crafted novel . . . drives home the point that everyday life is studded with memorable moments."—*Publishers Weekly*, starred review

★ "Holt has crafted a remarkable story about finding yourself by opening up to the people around you. An excellent choice to read alone or aloud."—*School Library Journal*, starred review

The Ambassador of Nowhere Texas

KIMBERLY WILLIS HOLT

Christy Ottaviano Books

Henry Holt and Company

New York

Henry Holt and Company
Publishers since 1866
120 Broadway
New York, NY 10271

mackids.com

Henry Holt books may be purchased for business or promotional use.
For information on bulk purchases, please contact Macmillan Corporate
and Premium Sales Department at (800) 221-7945 x5442 or by email at
specialmarkets@macmillan.com.

Library of Congress Cataloging-in-Publication Data

Names: Holt, Kimberly Willis, author.
Title: The ambassador of Nowhere Texas / Kimberly Willis Holt.
Description: First edition. | New York : Christy Ottaviano Books, Henry
    Holt Books for Young Readers, 2021. | Companion to: When Zachary
    Beaver came to town. | Audience: Ages 8–12. | Audience: Grades 4–6. |
    Summary: In 2001, seventh-grader Rylee Wilson and new student Joe,
    whose father was a New York City first responder on 9/11, decide to find
    Zachary Beaver and reunite him with Rylee's father, Toby.
Identifiers: LCCN 2020020577 | ISBN 9781250234100 (hardcover)
Subjects: CYAC: Best friends—Fiction. | Friendship—Fiction. | Family
    life—Texas—Fiction. | Texas—Fiction.
Classification: LCC PZ7.H74023 Amb 2021 | DDC [Fic]—dc22
LC record available at https://lccn.loc.gov/2020020577

First Edition, 2021

Printed in the United States of America by LSC Communications,
Harrisonburg, Virginia.

10 9 8 7 6 5 4 3 2 1

TO THE CHILDREN OF 9/11

Welcome to
ANTLER
IF YOU DON'T WANT SOMETHING TOLD,
DON'T TELL US!
POPULATION 856   ELEVATION 3,600

CHAPTER 1

My grandmother told me she once watched an abandoned house fold inside itself. The roof had caved in, leaving a hollow shell.

"A house needs people, Rylee," she claimed, "or it will die."

Every time I passed Miss Myrtie Mae's home, I watched for signs of the roof giving way or the walls collapsing. But even though ivory paint flakes covered the ground like snow and the roof had shed a few shingles, the old house looked as if it were holding its breath, waiting for someone to claim it.

When Miss Myrtie Mae was alive, her home used to be the grandest in town. Antler held their annual Easter egg hunt on her lawn. Every girl, including me, would wear her Sunday dress and white Mary Janes. The year Twig moved here was the last celebration. I'd always dreamed of finding the golden egg, but never did. Twig discovered it. Someone had hidden it in a hollow trunk at the property line.

After she died, Miss Myrtie Mae's house got the most attention on Halloween. Trick-or-treaters rushed past the place, believing it was haunted. And around midnight the Jerks—Vernon Clifton and his buddy Boone from my junior high—threw rocks at the windows. Dad said he once dreamed he saw Miss Myrtie Mae emerge from behind the lopsided screen door that hung from a single hinge. She was carrying a silver tray with her famous lime gelatin and turkey salad.

Four years after Miss Myrtie Mae died at the ripe old age of 101, Dad still mowed her lawn.

On a blistering hot day last summer, Mom told him, "Toby, you're crazy to keep doing that."

"I've mowed it since I was thirteen, Tara," he said. "Can't see a reason to stop now."

Later Mom told me it was those kinds of things Dad did that made her fall in love with him.

After last winter's snowstorm, icicles clung to Miss Myrtie Mae's house long after the sun had melted the snow everywhere else in town. Once on the way home from school, Twig and I watched the icicles drip and listened to the plopping sounds as they landed in puddles. I swear it looked like the house was crying.

By summer 2001, Miss Earline had posted a FOR SALE sign on the lawn. The lawyers in charge of Miss Myrtie Mae's estate had finally solved the new owner mystery. She surprised the whole town by leaving her home to a man who proposed to her many years ago. He'd broken it off after she wanted to postpone the wedding because her much older bachelor brother pretended to be on his deathbed.

Almost everyone in Antler thought she must have been crazy to have left the house to him, but my grandmother Opa said, "Miss Myrtie Mae was a wise woman. I think she was telling the world that she once had a great love. Maybe I'll write a song about it."

Turned out, the man had never married and he died a week after Miss Myrtie Mae, which Opa said made the whole thing even more tragically romantic.

The man's oldest great-grandniece from Brooklyn inherited the house. Since she'd never heard of Antler and had no plans to leave New York, she decided to sell it. She might have to wait a long time. There weren't many people calling Miss Earline to say they wanted to buy an old mansion in Antler.

~

Every summer I worked regular shifts at our family's snow cone stand. Since Mom and Dad were teachers, it was the perfect business. We always opened the week of spring break. Then it was weekends only until summer break, when we opened every day except Sunday.

Mom and Dad had good childhood memories of eating Bahama Mamas at Wylie Womack's stand, and they named our business Wylie's Snow Cones in honor of him. If you asked me, it was kind of the same as mowing a dead woman's lawn. How would Wylie Womack know? He was buried six feet under. Plus it was confusing when people from out of town stopped at the stand. They always asked if Wylie was my dad.

Even though I worked daily shifts all summer, I still had time to hang out with Twig. Most days we rode our bikes from the west side of town to the east side. Then we pedaled all the way back again.

The first round we spent half our time making tracks at Gossimer Pit. On our second lap we turned at the square that surrounded the courthouse, getting off our bikes to say hello to Ferris. He was always sitting on an old bread box out front of his Bowl-a-Rama Café. Ferris claimed he still ran the place, but really Samuel Pham did. Mr. Pham came to Texas from Vietnam almost thirty years ago. He worked in a lot of Amarillo restaurant kitchens before moving to Antler and living in a room at the back of the café. Now we could order pho and shrimp along with chicken-fried steak.

Ferris usually had a story or two to tell us. Twig and I had heard them before, including the scriptures he managed to slip in. We sat and listened anyway. I was just relieved Ferris was the forgiving type and wasn't sore at us for dropping out of the Tumbleweeds, a bowling league he'd started up for young people. I'd enjoyed being in the league, but when Twig quit because she thought ninepin bowling was pointless, I followed. Then the other kids started dropping out.

After Twig and I said our goodbyes to Ferris, we would finish our spin around the square. Then we wove through the back streets until we reached Allsup's, the convenience store that sat on Highway 287, and where Twig's mom worked as a cashier. We never failed to stop there for a Dr Pepper. Straddling our bikes, we sipped through our straws, watching people from other places headed in the direction of either Amarillo or Wichita Falls. Two years ago, when we were ten, we started keeping a list of the states on the license plates. We'd collected forty-nine so far, including Alaska, Hawaii, and Washington, DC. Apparently no one from Vermont or Maine wanted to visit the Texas Panhandle.

The license plate game wasn't the only one we played. Another was making up stories about the people who got out of their cars and went inside Allsup's. Twig was better at it than me, not because I didn't have an imagination, but because she was braver and could stare a long time at people. She studied them so hard she could soak up a bunch of details, from their aviator sunglasses propped atop their heads to their double-tied green shoelaces. Sometimes when people caught her staring, they glimpsed down at their pants as if they'd left their fly open. Sometimes they stared back at her. Twig didn't bat an eye.

That's the way it was with us last summer. But then everything changed. And when it did, I believed that Twig and I would never again talk about where all those people, going in and out of Allsup's, were heading.

ANTLER
PUBLIC LIBRARY
HOURS
TUES.-THUR.-FRI. 1:PM to 4:PM.

CHAPTER 2

The middle of August, Twig left with her grandmother and her cousin for Madrid. Her grandmother grew up there and moved to the United States when she was a child. Twig had always complained about her cousin, Cora, how she was shallow and only interested in clothes, makeup, and boys. More than once she told me, "I wish you were going instead."

I wished that, too, and secretly hoped Cora would get some awful throat infection or wake up with splotches all over her face and have to stay home in Dallas. Of course that didn't happen. And worse, as the date for the trip grew closer, I could tell Twig was excited about going, even if it meant she'd be around her snotty cousin. The trip meant Twig would miss the first two weeks of school. Her mom got permission from the principal, Mr. Arlo, who said, "Twig will learn more in Spain than the first ten days here."

My parents were teachers. Dad taught seventh- and eighth-grade history, and Mom taught speech and drama. They both had strong opinions about Mr. Arlo's decision.

Dad agreed with him, but Mom thought Mr. Arlo was setting a bad example. "What if every kid went out of town at the beginning of the school year?"

It wasn't that Mom was all seriousness and no play. Her old classmates called her Party Charlie. I figured Mom was like me, a little jealous. Going to Red River, New Mexico, a few years ago was the only real vaca- tion we'd ever had. Mom had always been envious of my aunt Scarlett's jet-setting life as a flight attendant. Aunt Scarlett had traveled to every state and now flew internationally. She owned a tiny apartment in Paris and had a French boyfriend who looked like a model.

The last three weeks of summer break, I went to the Antler Public Library in the courthouse basement, making my way again through the teen section. It consisted of two shelves. I loved rereading my favorites, but I'd practically memorized them. Twig visited our library just to use the computer. The Garcias were the only family I knew that owned one.

Now I also went to use the computer to check my email. The dial-up to connect was so slow, the train could make it through town quicker. The wait was worth it to see Twig's updates, even if they were short.

Hey, Rylee,
They eat dinner so late here, I'm always starving! Give me a Bowl-a-Rama burger and greasy fries.
PS: Cora is driving me crazy!
Trying to stay sane in Spain,
Twig

Dear Rylee,

Went to a bullfight. That poor bull! Come back with me and we'll protest. We'll take Cora, but let's leave her in Spain.

Bull Defender,

Twig

Rylee,

You should see my gorgeous cousin, Paulo. Last night he took me on a motorcycle ride after dinner. Too bad we're related.

Amor,

Twig

Aside from the emails, Twig sent one postcard—a picture of a tiny truck parked on a narrow cobbled street. On the back she'd scribbled, *How awesome would it be to drive this around Antler? Wish you were here. Stay cool, Twig.*

She was the cool one. It must have been rough, eating paella and hanging out with a handsome cousin every day. At least one of us was having a great end of the summer. Maybe she'd even get kissed. We talked about kissing a lot, wondering which of us would be first. Sometimes I daydreamed about a cute guy moving here, some guy who would pick wildflowers for me, like the Engelmann daisies that grew along the railroad track. Maybe he'd even kiss me in Mrs. McKnight's rose tunnel. But if he ever saw Twig, I wouldn't stand a chance.

The day before school started, I received another email from Twig.

Played soccer with my cousins in the street last night. They call it football here. Remember when you reinvented the game? See you in a couple of weeks!
Friends forever,
Twig

She was referring to her first day at Antler Elementary School, when I stupidly picked up the soccer ball during PE. I was only in second grade and never paid attention to soccer, but Coach Hayward made me feel like a fool, blowing her whistle until I dropped the ball. When I did, Twig grabbed the ball and ran like a quarterback.

She then tossed the soccer ball to another kid, who took off running too. Twig and I were best friends from that day on. It was only later that I found out she knew how to play. She'd been the star of her soccer team in the last town she lived in.

I wasn't the only one Twig had saved. In fifth grade Conner Cook broke his collarbone from falling off a horse. His neck brace caused him to resemble a turtle with his head poking out of a shell. Twig insisted on carrying his books to every class for him.

She claimed she got her temper from her dad and her love of gumbo from her mom. It was true that she loved a big bowl of gumbo, but she didn't have her dad's temper. She was beautiful—long brown hair, longer than my blond strands (we measured and compared each month). She had dark eyes, not like my boring hazel ones. Her caramel skin had freckles sprinkled across her cheeks. My pale round face looked like a full moon. Her two front teeth overlapped a little, but somehow on Twig, crooked teeth looked cute. I, on the other hand, had perfectly straight teeth, and it had gotten me nowhere. She was brave. Always acting on her dares. I guess that's why so many kids had wanted to be her friend. Twig was a magnet, and the rest of us, paper clips. Sometimes I wondered if my classmates had been my friends only because of my friendship with her.

The night before school started, I felt restless and almost reached in my closet for my mandolin. But I hadn't touched it in a year. Instead, I went outside.

Dad was in his office in the backyard, reviewing his lessons for the week. His office used to be my grandfather's shed where he raised Tennessee brown nose fishing worms. After Grandpa died, Dad moved a desk, chair, and a lamp in there. He tacked old Texas maps to the walls and piled stacks of books around the room. An amateur birder, he kept his worn copy of *Texas Birds* and binoculars on his desk. It was a cramped place, but Dad was on the small side, so it fit him just fine.

"How's it going, Rylee?" He adjusted the lampshade so it wasn't shining in my eyes and turned down the oldies station on his radio.

"Fine."

When I didn't say anything else, he closed his notebook, but not before marking his place with a pen.

"Looking forward to seventh grade?"

"Well, I wish Twig was going to be there."

"Rylee, Twig may not be here every day of your life. People come and go even when we don't want them to."

I wondered who he was talking about, because he'd seen his best friend practically every day of his life.

"Seventh grade is going to be great," he said. "Because you are."

I only wished everyone saw me the same way my dad did.

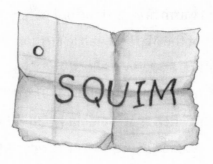

CHAPTER 3

Kids from three other small towns fed into our schools, which were all located in the same building. There were three different entrances: east—the elementary school, north—the high school, south—my junior high. If we'd had a west entrance, our school would have resembled a giant compass.

The first day of seventh grade, I walked the two blocks there with my six-year-old sister, Mayzee. The oatmeal Mom made us for breakfast settled like cement in my belly. A warm breeze came out of nowhere, bringing the stink of the Martins' cattle feedlot. My neck was still hot, so hot that for a quick moment, I wished I had short hair. Why hadn't someone made it a law for school to start when it was officially fall?

After we reached the schoolyard, Mayzee took off.

"Well, don't even say goodbye," I hollered to her.

"Bye!" she yelled, not bothering to glance back. I stood watching her disappear into the school, wishing I could have been like that—so happy to start the semester and meet up with friends. At her age, I'd always dreaded the first day filled with awkward moments—who to talk to before the bell rang, who to sit by at lunch.

When Twig and I became friends in second grade, we'd made up our own code words inspired by my chronic apologizing. Saying "sorry" was easy for me even if something wasn't my fault. If someone dropped a pencil or spilled juice, I apologized as if I'd done it myself.

Twig would catch me every time, and ask, "Why are *you* sorry?"

One day she said, "Don't say *sorry*, say *squim*."

Twig rarely, if ever, used *squim*, but it was the first of three words she'd invented. We used *tob* for anything awesome (like a cute guy or going to the movies) and *drin* if we dreaded doing something (like chores or going back to school after summer break). For a few years, we used our code words almost every day. Then somewhere around fifth grade, they'd slowly dropped from our vocabulary along with hopscotch and watching cartoons.

Just as I wondered if it would be a *tob* or *drin* kind of first day, a white Range Rover pulled up in front of the school, and the Garcia twins got out.

"Hey," I called to them.

Frederica waved. "Hi, Rylee!"

Her brother, Juan Leon, nodded toward me.

They were the smartest kids in my class, excelling in all subjects and under the spell of numbers. Even though we didn't hang out together, I'd known them all my life. If I was going to start seventh grade without Twig, at least I'd be able to sit in the cafeteria with Frederica and Juan Leon Garcia.

Juan Leon was named after his uncle, a professional golfer and our biggest celebrity from Antler. If it weren't for Tiger Woods winning all those tournaments, his uncle would probably have been even more famous.

Juan Leon wasn't anything like his uncle. When he talked about geometry problems or algebra, his nostrils flared and his thick eyebrows knitted together like they were digging their way to his brain. Sometimes I wondered how my fourth-grade self ever thought he was the cutest boy in Antler.

Frederica stood a head taller than Juan Leon. She was pretty, but seemed unaware of her looks. Most of the time she kept her long black hair pulled back in a low ponytail, and she never bothered shaving her legs even though she wore skirts.

In homeroom, I chose my locker midway down the hall. My homeroom teacher let me reserve the one next to mine for Twig. Everyone knew we were best friends, but with Twig gone, I was reminded of that all day. Kids came up to me and asked if I'd heard from her and if I knew when she was coming back from Spain. Even the Garcia twins broke away from their talk about Whiz

Quiz and asked if I was taking notes in the classes she was missing. I felt important. It made going to school without Twig a little easier. In the past when people came up to us, they looked her in the eyes when they spoke. Now I wasn't invisible. They were looking and talking to me.

CHAPTER 4

My grandmother Opa had moved to Nashville when Dad was about my age, hoping to make it big in country music. It didn't work out the way she'd dreamed. She recorded an album, but none of her songs were ever played on the radio.

When her second husband died, she returned home, bought the old Antler movie theater off the square, and opened Opalina's Opry House. It was a wreck, but my grandmother could put lipstick on a pig. Down came the raggedy blue curtains on the stage. Up went the red velvet ones. A huge chandelier hung in the center of the room, glittering the ceiling with light. Now on Saturday nights, Antler had a place to go for entertainment. Out-of-town Texas bands were the headliners, but Opa sang a song or two, and so did Mayzee.

Every Saturday morning since my little sister, Mayzee, was born, Opa and I had driven over to Amarillo to eat breakfast. She claimed it calmed her nerves for the big opry night.

The Saturday before Labor Day, Opa was due to arrive at our house. Since Mayzee was being her usual six-year-old bratty self, I waited outside on the porch. A few seconds later, Opa drove up in her pink convertible, named after an old country song. Delta Dawn had a bumper sticker that read I DON'T SELL MARY KAY COSMETICS.

Opa parked, waved, and hopped out of the car. As usual her short blond hair was teased high atop her head, resembling the pouf on a poodle's tail. It looked soft to the touch, but it was sprayed stiff to resist the strongest Panhandle wind. Some people might have thought her hairdo was a little outdated, but it matched her wardrobe, which consisted mainly of broom skirts, western blouses, and cowboy boots. She was a walking billboard for her opry, always leaving behind a flyer wherever we ate in Amarillo. I don't think anyone from there ever came, but who could blame Opa for trying?

That morning I started toward Delta Dawn, but Opa stopped me. "Hold on a minute, Rylee. I need to talk to your folks first. Follow me. You're not going to want to miss this."

The sign at our town's border should have read:

Welcome to Antler
Population 856
If You Don't Want Something Told, Don't
Tell Us!

Inside the house Mom and Dad were sitting at the kitchen table. Dad was like me, an early morning person. Dressed and shaved, he was reading the Amarillo paper. He also read the *Dallas Morning News* and the *New York Times*.

Mom was still wearing her short nightie. She had

nothing to hide. She worked out every day at the ladies' gym that was formerly Peggy Cartwright's barn, and she was Bronze Baby Tanning Salon's best customer. I wore pajamas to hide my buttermilk legs.

Mom didn't look happy when Opa chose a mug, poured herself some coffee, and plopped her huge purse down on the table, settling between them.

"You won't believe it!" Opa lifted the mug but didn't take a sip. "Miss Myrtie Mae Pruitt left a whole lot more than her house."

Mayzee abandoned her cartoons and jumped like a kangaroo into the kitchen. "I'm singing 'Candy Kisses.'"

I turned off her spotlight and asked, "Is the woman in New York going to get everything?"

"Oh, no, honey," Opa said. "Seems Miss Myrtie Mae has some packages that will be going to some of the citizens of Antler."

"Well, I sure hope she left us her gazebo," Mom teased.

Opa grabbed her purse and stood. "And that's not all."

She paused.

"Well?" Mom's eyes bulged.

"Seems we're going to have a brand-new library, thanks to our deceased benefactor."

That was a surprise, but it shouldn't have been. When Dad and Mom were kids, Miss Myrtie Mae was the town librarian. By the time I was born, she'd long since retired. Even then, she was willowy and stood erect as if someone had tied a board to her back. Her green eyes looked like prized marbles, and when she peered into anyone else's, it was as if she knew every lie they ever told. Her hair swirled like white cotton candy on top of her head and was held in place with a single pearl-trimmed comb. She spent her last years in bed, but before that, she walked around the square five times each morning, calling it her daily exercise. When I was a little girl I thought she was searching for something that she never seemed to find.

By Thursday at school, I'd heard that Ferris and old Sheriff Levi both received packages. I figured Dad didn't make the list. Then that afternoon, a UPS truck screeched to a stop in front of our house.

After the driver left, Dad stared at the package for a

long moment. Then he pulled out his pocketknife and ran the blade along the tape. An envelope was attached to something covered with white tissue paper that looked like a large picture frame. Or maybe it was one of Miss Myrtie Mae's cloudy mirrors.

In the envelope was a check for ten thousand dollars.

"Now we can go to Disney World!" Mayzee did her happy chicken jig around the kitchen, fists tucked under her pits, arms flapping, legs kicking. Her slippers flew through the air.

Dad tucked the check back into the envelope. "This is going into your college funds," he told us, quickly adding, "By the way, I don't want either one of you to brag about the money we received from Miss Myrtie Mae."

He focused on Mayzee.

"I won't," she said. "I'll just tell them."

"That's what he meant," I snapped. She was exhausting.

Dad knelt in front of Mayzee and gently cupped her shoulders. "Mayzee, you have to promise me, you won't tell *anyone* what Miss Myrtie Mae gave us."

"I promise." She batted her big baby blues. "Now open the other part."

My parents would have never let me get away with that tone.

"*Pleeeease*," she added, bouncing in place.

Dad tugged at the tissue paper. When it fell onto the floor, we stared at the framed photograph. There, in the middle of a cotton field, holding a sack, was the largest boy I'd ever seen.

CHAPTER 5

"Who is that fat boy?" Mayzee asked.

"Mayzee!" I said. "That's not nice."

"His name was Zachary." Dad kept studying the photograph. "Zachary Beaver."

"Do you know him?" I'd never heard Dad mention his name before.

"Years ago I did, but he didn't stay long in Antler. He was a sideshow boy."

"What's that?" asked Mayzee.

"They were shows that traveled with circuses. Right, Dad?" I'd read a book about circus history last summer.

He nodded. "Yep, or sometimes fairs. They don't have them anymore. Good thing, since it was nothing but a stare fest."

"But it's not nice to stare," Mayzee said.

"That's right, Mayzee," Dad said. "It's not nice to stare at people just because they're different."

"What do you mean?" Mayzee asked.

"Oh, maybe they could swallow swords," Dad said.

"Or bend their body into strange positions." I remembered the picture I saw of Pretzel Man.

"What did the fat boy do?" Mayzee asked.

"Mayzee!" I said.

"Nothing," Mom said, already bored. She headed toward the refrigerator and pulled out her snack container of carrot and celery sticks. "He just sat there, and people paid money to look at him. I think he was billed as the fattest boy in the world."

"Whoa!" Mayzee said. "In the whole wide world?"

Dad glanced up from the picture. "That's not all he was about."

"Like what?" Mom asked. She didn't believe a person should have an extra ounce of weight on their body.

"He liked to read. He loved travel books."

"Did you pay money to go see him, Dad?" I asked.

"Yeah, I'm ashamed to say I did."

Dad moved toward the living room with the picture.

Mom pointed a carrot stick at him. "Toby, don't hang it over the fireplace. That's where I plan to put my *Les Misérables* poster after I frame it."

For some reason, that ticked me off. We'd never had anything over our mantel since I could remember. She'd had that poster forever.

As usual, Dad obeyed her, placing the picture on the floor, leaning it against the wall, the image facing away from us.

"Why was he in the cotton field?" I asked.

Dad sank into the recliner with a newspaper. "It was the McKnights' farm. We used to release ladybugs at the end of summer so the bollworms didn't destroy the crop."

"You were there, too?" I asked.

"Yep."

"Was Uncle Cal?" Mayzee asked.

Dad nodded. "Of course."

Cal McKnight wasn't our real uncle. He and Dad grew up next door to each other and had been best friends forever. The McKnights still lived next door, but Uncle Cal lived in a mobile home at the end of their driveway. Now that Mr. McKnight was older, Uncle Cal was in charge of the cotton farm. Married and divorced a few times, he didn't have any kids, so I think he liked that we called him Uncle.

Mom had made her way to the kitchen and started chopping lettuce.

"Did you see him, Mommy?" Mayzee asked.

"Nah. I don't think so."

"Oh, yeah, you did," Dad said. "Your mom peed her pants when she saw him."

We laughed, and Mayzee fell back on the floor singing, "Mommy wet her pants, Mommy wet her pants!"

"I was only five or six." Mom acted miffed, but then she smirked.

"I'm six, and I don't wet my pants!" Mayzee said,

and then went back to "Mommy wet her pants! Mommy wet her pants!"

"Why was he in Antler?" I asked Dad.

"His sideshow was passing through town." He gazed across the room, his focus locked on the back of the picture. Then he picked up the *Amarillo Globe-News* and started to read like he wasn't interested in talking anymore. But he kept glancing over at the picture.

"I don't remember him being here that long," Mom said, "but I was so young. That kind of weight puts a lot of stress on your heart. I doubt he's still alive."

Dad lowered the paper and frowned. "You don't know that."

It all seemed like a mystery to me. "Why do you think Miss Myrtie Mae left you that photograph?"

"I have no idea, Rylee," Dad said. "Why did she leave her house to a man she hadn't seen in decades?"

If Miss Myrtie Mae had been as sharp as Opa believed, there must have been a reason she wanted Dad to have the photograph. I wanted to know everything about Zachary, but Dad became quiet. Maybe I wouldn't discover the reason that moment, but I was going to do my best to find out soon. Twig could help me when she returned. She'd probably notice a clue I'd missed. It wasn't every day that someone like Zachary Beaver came to our town.

CHAPTER 6

By Monday, school was buzzing about Miss Myrtie Mae's gifts. That would probably be trivial stuff in Amarillo or Dallas, but here, where everyone knows everyone, it was like having Christmas in September. The McKnights received a photograph of our street sign, Wayne McKnight Lane. Years ago, before I was born, our street was named Ivy Street, but it was later renamed in honor of Uncle Cal's big brother, who died in the Vietnam War. Uncle Cal told us he received a picture of a grocery sack on Zachary Beaver's trailer steps.

I kept my promise to Dad and didn't tell a soul. Even though I thought he really only meant the check, I didn't want to mention Zachary Beaver to anyone but Twig. Maybe she could unravel the mystery. Why had Miss Myrtie Mae given Dad and Uncle Cal photographs connected with Zachary?

That morning, Jerk 2, Boone Mavis, came over to my locker and leaned against Twig's. Like Jerk 1, Vernon Clifton, Boone had on a used army jacket. Unlike Jerk 1, he wore his hair in a long mullet. Sometimes when I saw him do something mean like tapping fifth graders on the backs of their heads, I wanted to say, *Billy Ray Cyrus called, and he wants his hair back.* Of course, I never did.

"How do y'all plan to spend all that money?" he asked.

"What?"

"The money that Miss Myrtie Mae left your family."

Mayzee Wilson had a big mouth. Friday night, when Uncle Cal was over for Lasagna Night, she dropped so many hints until she blurted out about the ten-thousand-dollar check.

But I acted dumb with Boone. "What are you talking about?"

"Oh, come on, everyone knows your family got a hundred thousand dollars."

Correction. Mayzee Wilson had a big *lying* mouth.

"My little sister has an imagination."

He scrunched up his face. "Your little sister?"

"Mayzee didn't tell you?"

Boone shook his mullet. "Nope. So I guess it's true, then."

"A hundred thousand dollars? Nope. It's not true, but who told you that, anyway?"

"My dad."

"Your dad?"

"Yeah, he was down at the café."

"The Bowl-a-Rama?"

He nodded. "He heard it from someone, Mr. McKnight, I think."

That made no sense. Mr. McKnight wasn't the type of person to gossip, even if he knew something.

"Not old Mr. McKnight," Boone added. "Cal McKnight."

Here I was blaming Mayzee, and Uncle Cal was the guilty one.

I shut my locker. "All I can say is you can't believe everything you hear. Plus you know he's always kidding around."

On the way to history class, two other kids asked me if the rumor was true. Each time I'd answer, "Geez, that's crazy."

I felt like a liar, even though I knew we hadn't inherited a hundred thousand dollars.

In class, Dad sat behind his desk, reading the Sunday *New York Times*. High Plains Public Radio played low in the background. The bell rang, and he folded the paper, then turned off the radio.

He took roll. I don't know why, but it kind of embarrassed me whenever he called out "Rylee Wilson." Maybe because Vernon Clifton usually made a crack or cradled and rocked his thick arms in front of his chest, reminding everyone that the teacher was my dad.

The biggest kid in our class, Vernon had failed fifth

grade and still struggled, which was probably why he tried to act so tough. I was an easy target.

This was the first year I was in Dad's class, but I'd have him again next year since he taught eighth-grade history, too.

Dad started his talk. He believed history was about people, and he moved through important events in the twentieth century by introducing them. He told us, "You won't care about World War I if the folks who made a difference don't matter to you."

Dad spoke with passion. I could get caught up in his lessons because he made you think you were there. Sometimes he asked Mom to role-play a historical figure in front of our class. We'd seen her play Eleanor Roosevelt and Susan B. Anthony. She was like watching a movie. She was so good, I'd forget she was my mom. And when I did remember, my throat got a funny tickle in it because I was so proud that she was.

As Dad made his opening remarks that day, Vernon's arm shot straight up while he peered at me sideways.

My stomach ached, thinking of what he might ask that would humiliate me.

Dad nodded in his direction. "Yes, Mr. Clifton?"

"Mr. Wilson, why are you still teaching this class?" Vernon smirked and took in all the other students.

It would be worse than I'd ever imagined. Vernon was going to point out the obvious. That it wasn't right for Dad to be my teacher. Dad actually went out of his way not to praise me in front of my classmates. But there were little things that he probably didn't realize he was doing that set me apart, like the way he addressed everyone by their last name except for me.

Dad shifted his body on the stool so that he was facing Vernon. "What's that, Mr. Clifton?"

"You know," Vernon said, "it's like you won the lottery."

"Excuse me?" Dad was confused, but I'd figured out exactly where this was going.

"A million bucks is a lot of money," said Vernon.

I nearly fell out of my chair. Some kids laughed nervously, but all of them leaned forward.

Ten thousand dollars turned into a hundred thousand by this morning, and now, less than an hour later, a hundred thousand had grown into a million bucks.

Zeros must have been dropping from the sky over Antler.

"Yes, it is a lot of money," Dad said. "But since I don't have a million bucks, I guess I'll show up here and teach history. Which reminds me, Mr. Clifton, report topics are due next week. We're looking forward to hearing what you've chosen to write about."

That shut Vernon right up. He always dreaded reading aloud.

I couldn't understand why Dad put up with Vernon's mouthing off, but Dad believed Vernon was a victim of circumstance. A couple of years ago, he set fire to trash dumpsters around town every twenty minutes until he was caught. We were a one-fire-engine town with volunteer firefighters. Whenever we heard a siren, Twig and I jumped on our bikes and rode until we reached the action. It didn't happen very often.

Vernon's dad, Mr. Clifton, volunteered and was one of the firefighters extinguishing the fires. When the sheriff's car drove up with Vernon in the back seat, Mr. Clifton yelled for his son to get out. Vernon sank lower as if he wanted to disappear. So Mr. Clifton marched away from the smoking dumpster, opened the back door, reached in, and grabbed Vernon by the ear, pulling him out of the vehicle.

I couldn't stand to watch any longer and turned away, but Twig looked on with tears in her eyes. I'd never seen her cry. Later she blamed it on the smoke, but I knew better because I'd wanted to do it myself.

In a big city, someone might have gone to juvenile hall for a stunt like that, but Vernon's punishment was to pick up trash at the square every day for two months.

After what happened with Mr. Clifton, I told Dad that I thought Vernon's dad was mean.

Dad set me straight. "I'm afraid we didn't always treat his dad right when we were kids. Back then, it seemed harmless, but over the years, I've realized it probably hurt Malcolm more than we knew. There were a couple of other guys who were tough on him too. Cal and I moved on, but the other guys never let up."

"You and Uncle Cal were bullies?"

Dad cleared his throat before answering. "It wasn't our usual way. We thought we were only pulling a couple of pranks, but in hindsight, it was mean-spirited.

Malcolm was humiliated by what Vernon did. I think it opened up some old wounds. Caused him to take his anger out on his son."

After he told me that, I figured that was why Dad put up with Vernon. He may have not been picking up trash at the square, but Dad was serving his own time.

We Remember
9-11-01

CHAPTER 7

It was September 11, and things would finally be getting back to normal. Twig was due to fly home on the twelfth. The last few nights, I tossed and turned from excitement. Instead of waking before the alarm went off like usual, I hit the snooze button twice, and might have pressed once more, but Mom was on the other side of my door, saying, "Rylee, I just woke up. Make Mayzee some oatmeal."

I almost said, *I just woke up, too,* but didn't. It

wouldn't have made a difference. Mom took forever getting ready—hot rollers, full makeup, manicure touch-up.

Why couldn't we eat Cap'n Crunch or Pop-Tarts like everyone else? Instead we had to eat slow-cooked lumpy oatmeal with chopped apples.

Mayzee followed me downstairs, both of us still wearing pajamas. Already dressed in his khakis and white shirt, Dad sat at the kitchen table, paying bills.

"I hope one of you girls becomes a plumber," he said, tearing a check from his checkbook.

While I stirred oats into the boiling water, Mayzee insisted on giving me a solo performance of the songs she planned to sing for Saturday's opry night.

"And then I'm going to twirl around." She stretched high on her tipped toes and twirled in place.

She continued to ramble. "And everyone will think that I'm finished, but I won't be. I'll sing—"

"Get dressed!" I snapped.

The oatmeal swam in the pot of water. I stirred and stirred. I still had to slice the fruit.

"But I'm not finished."

"I'm not even dressed," I said. "Go!"

Dad closed the checkbook. "Rylee, you can get ready, and I'll finish the oatmeal."

I dropped the wooden spoon on the counter, not even thanking him.

Mayzee turned her attention to her new audience. "Daddy, do you want to hear what I'm going to sing?"

"Mayzee," I yelled. "Go get dressed! You're going to make me late for school."

Upstairs, Mom stuck her head out of the hall bathroom, half of her hair rolled and half untouched. "Rylee, stop shouting."

"I'm going to be late!" I said.

"You're not going to be late," Mom said. "You've never been late a day in your life." She made it sound like a character flaw.

"Why don't you get up earlier so I don't have to do your job?" The words slipped out before I could stop them. For a split second, I felt great. She overslept at least twice a week and depended on me to take up the slack.

Mom shook a hot roller at me. "Excuse me, young lady, but I'll remind you, I'm your mother."

Then why don't you act like it? I wanted to say, but I bit my tongue, slamming my bedroom door behind me instead.

On the way to school, I stayed silent while Mayzee chattered about what she'd wear at the Saturday opry night. I didn't *ooh* and *ah* like I usually did when she described her outfits, this time a black western shirt with pink flamingos and fringe. Her closet was crammed with outfits from Amarillo's Boot and Spur.

We were almost at school when she stopped talking and looked up at me. "Are you mad?"

I stayed tight-lipped.

"Do you wish you still played the mandolin?"

For some reason, her question made me more irritated. "No," I snapped. "Now, hurry off to school or you'll be late."

She took off. Halfway to the entrance, she stopped, turned around, dashed back, and wrapped her skinny arms around my hips. I stood there stiff as burnt bacon. Then Mayzee sprinted off, crossing the field until she reached one of her many friends.

My first class, language arts, had only just started

when Mr. Arlo's voice came over the speaker. "Team A teachers, head to the office immediately." Our teacher, Mrs. Webb, left the room.

The last time I'd heard an announcement like that was when I was in fifth grade and an inmate from the Amarillo prison had escaped. Back then, the principal had announced, "Lockdown."

Mrs. Webb returned a few minutes later, her face white and the space above her mouth moist with perspiration.

Then Mr. Arlo announced for Team B teachers to report to his office. Mrs. Webb told us the World Trade Center Towers in New York had been hit by planes. She turned on the television, but said anyone who didn't want to watch could go to the cafeteria and read.

No one left the room.
We watched.
Planes crashing.
Flames and smoke.
Firefighters,
Police officers,

Men and women,

Running,

Yelling,

Crying,

Sirens.

We watched.

Replay.

The planes crashing.

Flames and smoke.

Firefighters,

Police officers,

Men and women,

Running,

Yelling,

Crying,

Sirens.

We kept watching.

I touched my desk,

My notebook,

My pen,

To feel something real.

But what we watched was real, too.

Someone muttered, "Kate McKnight." Uncle Cal's sister had lived in New York for years, working as a costume designer. Now I searched for Kate's face.

Then I remembered Twig. She was due back tomorrow. Would she be flying through New York?

The scenes of the planes crashing into the towers kept replaying on television. I closed my eyes, remembering Mayzee, her thin arms hugging me. I left the room, hurrying down our hall, making a left toward the elementary wing, passing the fifth-grade classes, fourth, and third. Outside the second-grade classes, the teachers had posted students' stories about their summer on the hallway walls. *We went to the beach*, said one. And when the essays changed into small rainbow-painted handprints, I slowed down until I reached Mayzee's first-grade classroom.

Staring into the door's small window, I surveyed the room for Mayzee. "All the Pretty Little Horses" was playing on a CD player.

When you wake, you shall have . . .

"Mayzee, where are you?" I whispered.

All the pretty little horses . . .

I scanned each row. Mayzee, Mayzee.

And then I saw her. She was in the front row, coloring. They were all coloring.

Way down yonder in the meadow . . .

I stood there watching, not wanting to leave. Then I turned and made my way back to my class. I'd only been gone a moment, and the television was now saying the Pentagon had been hit by another plane.

The bell rang just as the South Tower collapsed. Instead of hurrying out of the room, everyone sat frozen.

"Go ahead to your next class," Mrs. Webb said.

My legs felt heavy as I moved down the hall through the quiet. How could one hour change everything? How could I feel safe at the beginning of class and terrified by the end of it? It was as if someone had yanked a sturdy door off its hinges.

When I entered history class, Dad and I exchanged glances. It took every bit of effort to keep from clinging to him, but I obeyed the unspoken rule. When my teacher happened to be my parent, I had to act like they weren't, even if everyone knew it. Even if the world was coming to an end.

Walking between the rows, Dad took attendance. As he passed my desk, his hand touched my shoulder. It was so quick, I wondered if it happened. But I knew that it had. And for the rest of the class, I clung to that moment. Replayed it like that morning's news coverage.

Dad kept the television on, and when it was announced that a plane had crashed in Pennsylvania, two girls left the room crying. Dad turned the TV off.

"Turn it back on, Mr. Wilson." Vernon Clifton leaned forward, his chin resting on his fists.

"We've had enough for today, Mr. Clifton."

Dad told us to use the remainder of the hour silently reading from our textbook. But the words blurred, the letters transforming into people running and crying, buildings collapsing, again and again. I thought about Kate in New York and Twig on a plane and what happened before school, what I'd said to Mom.

At lunch I searched for her in the teachers' lounge, but she wasn't there. Then I headed to her classroom, where I found her and Dad, their backs to me. Dad's arm was around Mom's shoulders, and her head rested against him as they gazed out the window at Mayzee swinging on the playground. Before they could hear or see me, I backed away and went to the cafeteria, settling across the table from the Garcia twins.

We were quiet as we ate bites of beef stew and stole glances at the big clock that hung above the double doors. It was as if we were waiting for something big to happen that would prove the morning had not been real after all.

A few parents came to school, picked up their kids, and took them home. The rest of the day felt meaningless, like we were weaving in and out of classrooms as clocks marked off the seconds.

The last bell for the day finally rang, and I waited for Mayzee outside in our usual spot. When I saw her exit the building, I hurried across the grass, picked her up, and squeezed her.

Her shoes hit my knees as I spun her around, and she repeated what she'd started to tell me that morning. "And I'll twirl exactly like this, and the audience will think I'm done, but I won't be. I'll sing another song."

"And you'll be so great!" I told her, still hugging her tight, trying to hold on to one good moment in this awful day.

After my parents got home, Mom called Aunt Scarlett. I'd forgotten all about her. Now I had one more person to worry about, but Mom found out she was at home in Paris and wasn't scheduled to fly until next month.

I rode my bike to Allsup's to see Twig's mom, but another cashier told me Mrs. Wagner had been upset and left earlier that day. I raced home to call her.

"She's okay, Rylee," Mrs. Wagner said. "I finally was able to reach her. Her grandmother's not sure when they'll be able to fly home, but they're safe at her great-aunt's. That was so nice of you to check on her."

Later Dad told me it might be a while before Twig made it home. Planes were all grounded in the United States and would have to wait until the FAA cleared international flights. Uncle Cal told us Kate was all right, too. The McKnights wanted her to rent a car and drive home, but Kate said she was fine and would see them at Christmas.

After Mayzee went to bed, Dad turned on the television and told me I was welcome to watch.

But I told him, "No, thanks. I'm sleepy."

I wasn't, but I needed to be in my room. To see

everything the way I left it that morning, before everything happened. My unmade bed, my favorite books stacked in the corner, and my signed poster of my favorite group, Nickel Creek. They were a trio that had played together since they were younger than me and were barely out of their teens now. Sara Watkins played the fiddle and sang like an angel, and her brother, Sean, was a talented guitarist. Chris Thile was one of the best mandolin players in the world. The way their voices and instruments blended on "Sweet Afton" caused a chill to slip down my spine.

Opa had given me the poster. She had a friend who had a friend who knew a guy who owned a place where they performed. The poster used to hang over my bed, but when Twig teased me about it, I hung it on the inside of the closet door. Even though Twig went to the opry every Saturday night, she didn't like bluegrass or country. She was a Weezer fan to the core.

I opened my closet door and pulled the mandolin off the shelf. The pick was still in the penny jar where I'd dropped it the last time I played. My fingers pressed the strings in the frets, remembering how to make the

G, C, and D chords. The calluses I'd started to get on my fingertips a year ago had softened, and my wrist hurt from not practicing for so long. There were a lot of songs I could play with just those three chords, which was a good thing, because I'd never been able to accomplish bar chords to my liking. Using the pick, I strummed "This Land Is Your Land," one of the first songs Opa taught me.

When I'd told Opa I wanted to learn to play the mandolin, she'd been so happy she could have clicked her cowboy boots together and shot like a rocket to the moon. She taught me to play and gave me her dad's, my great-grandfather's, mandolin. The gift meant a lot to me, not just because it had been his or because it was a Gibson mandolin from the 1930s, but because Opa had wanted me to have it. She never said anything, but I could tell she was disappointed when I stopped wanting to learn.

Mom knocked on my door and popped her head inside my room. "You okay?"

"Yes," I said softly.

She smiled. "You're playing again?"

"Nah," I said. "Just goofing around."

"I wish you'd goof around more often," she said. "I miss your playing."

As she started to ease the door shut, I called to her. "Mom?"

The door opened wide, and Mom stayed in the doorway, her small frame backlit by the hall light.

"Yes?"

I swallowed. "I'm sorry . . . about this morning."

"I know, pumpkin. Love you."

Then she shut the door.

～

It was way after midnight when our phone rang. At first I thought I was dreaming and then I remembered everything that had happened since the morning and my heart began to race.

A moment later, there was a soft tapping on my door, and before I could say anything, Dad had opened it. He spoke in a hushed tone. "Rylee, someone's on the phone for you."

I picked up my phone, the one I'd received for my

birthday, when I'd wanted a private line but got an extension instead.

"Hello?"

"Rylee? It's me. Twig."

"Twig!"

"I can't talk long. My mom said you called, and I just wanted to let you know I'm okay. How are you doing?"

And even though I'd held it together all day, I burst into tears.

ESTATE
SALE

Saturday, September 15
8:00 am - 6:00 pm
All proceeds will go to
the new Antler Public Library

BURGESS AUCTION HOUSE

CHAPTER 8

Only two days had passed since the terrorists attacked. Flags started waving in every Antler yard like they did on Memorial Day, Flag Day, and the Fourth of July. At the post office and courthouse, they flew half-mast. The Bowl-a-Rama Café was now painted red, white, and blue. Ferris said it was Mr. Pham's idea and that he was still busy stenciling stars on the roof.

Miss Earline bought hundreds of tiny flags and put them on the grounds around the square. Of course she also put a tag on each with her phone number that read EARLINE'S REAL ESTATE. BUY OR SELL. CALL ME.

Reverend Colfax led a prayer circle each morning in front of the courthouse at seven, and most of the town showed up. Between noon and one, the mayor piped patriotic music from the courthouse. It was so loud we could hear it during school lunch a quarter of a mile away.

Opa considered canceling Saturday's show, but decided to open with "The Star-Spangled Banner" and end the night's performance with "Oh, Beautiful."

~

The sky remained eerily silent on the days that followed, because no planes were allowed to fly into, out of, or within the United States. School wasn't quiet, though. The attacks were the only thing people wanted to talk about. Some of my classmates claimed they hated the terrorists and didn't trust any Muslims. Vernon Clifton mouthed off about how he wished he could chain Osama bin Laden, the leader of al Qaeda, behind his dad's Jeep and drag him across Texas. Some of the same kids who talked about how much they hated Muslims made their own prayer circles before school the days following the attacks. To me, it didn't seem right to act like it was okay to hate and then turn around and pray for peace.

For the first few days, our school held a moment of silence each morning in remembrance of those who died on September 11. We also had surprise lockdown and fire drills. Mr. Arlo was out for a district meeting and left our anxious vice principal, Ms. Lamb, in charge. She announced continuous drills. Just about the time we returned to our seats and the teacher started back teaching, Ms. Lamb would announce another one. Some of the kids said the reason she kept sounding the alarm was because Pantex, a nuclear facility, was located near our town.

"We could be next," Vernon said as if he were a government authority.

Doing anything seemed pointless, even brushing my teeth. What did it matter if my molars turned black and fell out when so many people had lost their lives? All conversations seemed to lead to one thing—what had happened that Tuesday. In bed when I closed my eyes, all I could see was the Twin Towers crumbling. I just wanted to see Twig walking into our school building safe and sound.

Then, Friday, a sign went up in Miss Myrtie Mae's yard.

ESTATE SALE
SATURDAY, SEPTEMBER 15
8:00 A.M.–6:00 P.M.
ALL PROCEEDS WILL GO TO
THE NEW ANTLER PUBLIC LIBRARY
BURGESS AUCTION HOUSE

~

Some people talked about how the timing was in bad taste. They believed they should postpone it, but the auction company said they were booked for months and warned us that people from all over the Panhandle would show up anyway. So the auction happened as scheduled.

Opa bought a Victrola to display in the opry house lobby. Mom secretly bought Miss Myrtie Mae's camera after seeing Dad admire it. She said she'd hide it until his birthday. And when I discovered an unmarked box of used film rolls, I hurried with it to the cashier.

"There's no price for these," I told her.

She peered through her glasses at the box, gave it a good look-over. "Where was it?"

"In the parlor next to the camera." I had five dollars in my pocket, so I was hoping it wasn't a cent more.

"You do know the film is already used, right?"

"Yes, ma'am," I said.

"Did you know Miss Pruitt?"

"Yes, ma'am. My dad mowed her lawn, and she's our neighbor. I mean, *was* our neighbor. My mom is the lady who bought the camera."

She smiled. "I think it was supposed to go with the camera. So I guess it belongs to your mom."

"Thank you!"

I hurried home with my prize, where Opa was waiting out front on the porch. I showed her the film.

"Oh, I love a good mystery. Since it's later than usual," she said, "I thought we'd go to brunch."

"Can we drop the film off at a drugstore first?"

"I'm counting on it!" Opa said. "I'll bet they'll be

finished developing them by the time we're done eating."

I couldn't wait to see what the pictures would reveal. Maybe there'd be more of Zachary Beaver.

Unfortunately all fourteen rolls revealed either items inside Miss Myrtie Mae's bedroom or views outside of her window, probably taken when she was bedridden her last year. I shuffled through them quickly, but hairbrushes, bird feeders, and other things like that can be pretty boring stuff to look at. A self-portrait with Miss Myrtie Mae staring back in the mirror seemed to be the only interesting one.

Remembering the drugstore's film policy, I said, "Opa, we don't have to pay for these if we don't want them. Well, maybe I'll keep the self-portrait."

"Keep them all," she said. "They may mean something to you one day."

I didn't see how, but I slipped the photos back into the bag.

CHAPTER 9

It was September 20. Twig arrived the day before, but she didn't call me. "She's probably catching up on sleep," Dad said. "There's a seven-hour time difference."

Still I was hurt, but then I remembered how she called me late on September 11. On the walk to school, I thought about everything she'd missed—finding the owner of Miss Myrtie Mae's house, the new future library, the Bowl-a-Rama Café's new look, and especially about Zachary Beaver. There was so much to tell her.

At school, I waited for her by our lockers, rearranging my textbooks a million times, hearing the slams of other locker doors. I felt dumb standing there, so I decided to make a quick WELCOME BACK, TWIG sign and taped it to the front of her locker.

Vernon and Boone came over and checked out the sign. Then Vernon dug a pen from his backpack and signed his name, but not before he wrote, *Hey, Hot Stuff, Missed you!* He handed the pen to Boone, who scribbled his signature.

Jerks! I mouthed to the floor when they walked away. A few other kids stopped by to read the sign. They asked if they could add their names, too, and I told them sure, even handing them my own pen.

A minute before the first bell was about to ring, kids were still signing, including the Garcia twins.

Handing back my pen, Frederica nudged me and tilted her head toward the entrance. "There she is."

At first I didn't recognize Twig. Her long hair had been cut into a pixie, and she wore black mascara and deep rose lipstick.

Every girl in the main hall, except Frederica and

me, rushed to Twig, squealing over her new appearance. They swarmed to her like little kids surrounding an ice cream truck.

Frederica left for homeroom. "See you later."

I moved closer to Twig, waiting for my turn.

Then the bell rang and everyone scattered off to homeroom, leaving the two of us. We hugged.

"Hey," Twig said, but her confident, upbeat tone was missing.

"Is everything okay?" I asked.

She frowned. "Yeah. Why do you ask?"

"No reason." I thought about what Dad said about the seven-hour difference. She was probably sleepy.

"Your locker is right next to mine," I told her. "Mrs. Frank let me choose it."

Instead of saying, "Cool" or "Awesome," like Twig would have, she followed me in silence.

When she saw the paper, she muttered, "That was nice."

"I didn't get a chance to sign it."

She pulled the sign off and stuck it inside her empty

locker. We headed to our homerooms together, but it felt like I was walking alone.

At lunch we sat by Frederica and Juan Leon. It wouldn't have seemed right not to. I'd sat with them every day since the beginning of school. Juan Leon broke away from his math talk with Frederica to ask Twig about the flight.

"Was there extra security?"

"Yeah, I guess," she said. "Yeah, there was."

"Were there long lines?"

"Mm-hm."

"Suitcase searches?"

"Mm-hm."

"Pat downs?"

She sighed. "Yep. It was definitely different flying home than leaving."

"I heard there were undercover security as passengers. Did you see any?" Juan Leon asked.

Frederica rolled her eyes. "Well, if they were undercover, she wouldn't know, would she?"

He lifted his thick eyebrows. "Well, she might have suspected."

"Stop interrogating her," Frederica said. I was glad she'd said it.

Juan Leon went on to defend his questions by explaining deductive reasoning, using a math problem to demonstrate his point.

That's when I zoned out. Twig had too and was breaking her potato chips into tiny pieces, none of them making their way to her mouth. She seemed to be more than sleepy. Something was bothering her. Probably September 11 or Juan Leon's questions about it.

~

After school, Twig said, "I've been thinking. Let's ride our bikes to the canyon overlook Friday."

"This Friday?" We were off Friday because of a teacher-in-service day, but she could have said any day. The canyon overlook was more than twenty miles away, and there was a steep, twisting incline to cycle up before reaching it.

"I should have known," Twig said. "You're never going to do it, are you?"

Even though I knew Mayzee was spending the night with Opa Thursday night and they were rehearsing Friday for Saturday's opry, I said, "My parents might need me to watch Mayzee."

That wasn't the first time Twig had asked me to ride with her to the canyon overlook. The last time was during last summer break when we were bored. But I'd made up some excuse then too.

"You're afraid," she'd said.

She was right. What would my parents say if I asked to pedal over twenty miles out of town? They'd never give me permission to go. I'd have to lie to them.

"Next summer would be better," I told her, secretly hoping she'd forget.

"Sure," she said, but her tone said it all. She hadn't believed me.

Now a big chunk of silence wedged between us as we waited for Mayzee. Kids exited the school like a stirred anthill, some heading to buses and cars, others to the road to walk home.

"Well, I'm going," Twig said.

Mayzee ran out of the school and joined us.

"Twig!"

And for a split second Twig was her old self. A broad smile crossed her face, and she hugged Mayzee. "Hey, short stuff. Was first grade ready for you?"

At home in the kitchen, Mom asked, "How's Twig doing?"

"Fine." Then I added, "I don't know. Something seems wrong."

"She didn't tell you about her parents splitting up?"

My body went numb. "What? How did you find out?"

Mom gave me her you-should-know look but said it anyway. "We live in Antler."

At least now I understood why Twig was acting different. But knowing it made me feel worse, because I thought since I was her best friend, she would have leaned on me, instead of building a wall between us.

I shouldn't have been surprised. Mr. Wagner had a bad temper. A couple of summers ago, I'd spent the night at Twig's house. We were playing checkers in her bedroom when her father started yelling at her mother in the next room.

A few seconds later, we heard the front door slam,

followed by his pickup truck screeching out of the driveway, then puttering down the road.

I peered at Twig across the checkerboard. Her eyes were empty, the way she looked when something happened that would cause most kids to break down.

My parents had never fought beyond a small spat, but I wanted to make her feel better. "My parents argue sometimes, too."

She stared hard at me, frowning. Then with a flat tone, she tapped the checkerboard with her index finger and said, "Your turn."

Her dad came back an hour later with a gallon of Blue Bell Homemade Vanilla ice cream. Her mother never came out of the bedroom, but we watched her dad fill up big bowls while we awkwardly laughed at his stupid jokes. I'd been so excited to finally be asked to spend the night at her house, but as her father spooned perfect round scoops of ice cream, I'd never felt so homesick. Maybe to Twig, riding to the canyon overlook was an escape from her parents' breakup. Probably she just wanted to do something they wouldn't approve of.

I picked up the phone and dialed her number.

"Okay. I'll do it," I told her.

"Do what?" she asked.

"I'll ride to the overlook with you on Friday."

CHAPTER 10

"Do you think we'll be back by dark?" I asked Twig the next day.

"Of course we will. I figured it out. It'll take us half a day to get there and half a day back. If we leave right after breakfast, we can pack a lunch and eat it at the overlook. Then we'll turn back and arrive home before dinner."

Twig's plan started to sound convincing. Besides, the long ride would give her a chance to finally open up to me about her parents, and I could tell her about Zachary Beaver.

Friday, I told my parents Twig and I would be riding bikes all day. I didn't say where. They didn't question me either. It wasn't a lie, but why did it feel like one? Riding bikes was really what we did most of the time together anyway.

At eight that morning, we met at Allsup's. Outside Twig handed me a bottle of water to add to my backpack. "Here, you'll need this."

I was nervous and excited as we breezed past the town limits, heading south on the old highway. The road was quiet, but it wasn't traveled much, mainly ranchers and cotton farmers heading to and from home. The sky was overcast, and the wind kicked at the prairie grasses.

"Don't look back," Twig said. "You'll turn into a pillar of salt."

After a while, I couldn't help it. I glanced over my shoulder and saw Antler's cotton gin. Aside from the water tower, it was our town's tallest structure. Now it looked like a silver thimble on the horizon. The sky was getting darker too, just like it did before a huge summer storm.

Thirty minutes into the ride, my legs already ached. They hurt more when I thought of the long journey ahead, the steep, winding road leading to the wall of the canyon we'd have to pedal up before reaching the overlook.

An unfamiliar truck passed us, pulling over to the left side of the road to give us plenty of room. We raised our arms in a wave. After the truck disappeared, the only sound for a while was the *clink-clunk* of a nearby windmill.

The sky kept getting darker, but I didn't dare mention it. I'd protested enough. A mile down the road, tiny little pellets hit our bodies. It had started to hail.

"Ping," Twig said every time they hit her like bullets bouncing off Superman. She kept pedaling.

Ping. Ping.

The road looked as if it were covered in rock salt. We pedaled slower, making crunching sounds with our tires. There was no dodging them. I scanned the area and discovered a cowshed in an old cotton field. We rode over to the fence and carefully crawled through the barbed wire, abandoning our bikes on the other side as we hurried for shelter.

The hail stopped, but was followed by sheets of rain that thumped loudly on the metal roof. We watched awhile in silence, then we shared our plans about what we would do when we grew up and graduated from Antler High.

"I'm going to travel everywhere by backpack," Twig yelled over the heavy rain.

I cupped my hands together. "After college?"

"The world will be my college. While you're studying your old dusty textbooks, I'll be learning from life."

I didn't say anything.

"You can come too," she added.

"Okay," I lied. "Sounds like a plan."

Twig smiled, but the twitch in her eyes revealed that she didn't believe me. Mom and Dad had brainwashed me about going to college since I could walk. I kind of wanted to go anyway.

I wondered when she was going to tell me about her

parents, but she didn't. So I asked her about Madrid. She answered, but the excitement she showed in her postcards was missing. It was as if she'd only gone down the road to Childress.

The hard rain slowed, turning into a gentle sprinkle, and Twig still hadn't said anything about the breakup. Then I asked her, "Were your parents glad to see you back home?"

She squinted at me. "Of course."

I quickly changed the subject. "You need to see the photograph Miss Myrtie Mae left my dad."

I went on, telling her all I knew about Zachary Beaver, how other people in town received pictures that had to do with the time he was here, and how I was determined to find out the importance of his visit and hoped she'd help.

"Why else would Miss Myrtie Mae give him that picture?" I asked.

Twig didn't answer. She didn't even seem interested. Then she leaned back against the wall of the cowshed and said, "I got kissed in Madrid."

"Really?"

"And again and again, and again. Two different guys, both friends of my cousin Paulo."

"On the same day?"

She laughed. "No! Not on the same day."

Suddenly my whole talk about Zachary seemed silly and childish. I wished I'd never mentioned him. My gut had a gnawing feeling that had nothing to do with hunger. It wasn't that I ever believed I'd be the first. Deep down I'd always figured that it would be Twig.

The rain stopped, and for a moment we lingered, waiting to see if it would start again. When it didn't, we went to get our bikes. Twig looked south, and I looked north.

"Well, we almost made it." I tried to sound disappointed.

"What do you mean?" Twig asked. "Nothing's changed. For me, anyway."

I stared at the spot where my bicycle tire touched the road.

"I knew you wouldn't finish," she said, positioning her bike in the direction of the overlook.

"It was hailing. It might start up again." The clouds

still made a thick charcoal cover above us. September was the time of the year when twisters could appear out of nowhere.

"Go on," Twig said. Then she hopped on her bike and pedaled in the direction of the overlook.

The gray sky looked like it was pouting, ready to let loose again. She was right. I was afraid. I watched her for a long while, trying to find the courage to follow. Instead I turned and pedaled in the opposite direction, heading toward Antler, heading toward home.

CHAPTER 11

The clouds didn't clear. At the square, I thought about turning on Main Street and stopping at the opry to see Opa. But she, Mayzee, and the other performers would be rehearsing for the next night's show. All I really felt like doing anyway was being alone in my room. Things had changed between Twig and me. Maybe forever.

When I arrived home, no one was there. My parents must have still been at school. At least I wouldn't have to answer any questions about where I'd been.

A minute later, I heard Dad drop his keys down on the kitchen counter. He walked into the living area and smiled when he saw me, looking relieved.

"There you are," he said. "Nasty hailstorm. You weren't out in it, were you?"

"I found quick cover."

"Good. Hey, want to help me pick some new flavors for next year?"

"Sure."

He handed me the catalogue. People wouldn't believe how many snow cone syrup flavors there are to choose from. Some make me want to puke just reading them, like Honey Pickle Juice and Burnt Marshmallow. Little kids would probably love them, though.

I continued reading down the page, but after a minute, the names wouldn't sink in. My thoughts were on Twig. I kept an ear out for the phone. An hour passed, and I thought about calling Twig's house, but if I did and her mom answered and Twig wasn't there, she'd worry because she thought Twig was with me.

After I made a list of my syrup choices for Dad, I

went to my room. I tried to read, but couldn't concentrate. Then I thought about working on my report for Dad's class, but ended up cleaning out my closet instead. This was Dad's bedroom growing up, and occasionally I was reminded of it when I discovered something like a toy soldier in the bottom drawer or the scribbled note on the back of the closet wall. In pencil, he'd written, *Right Hand Man Muscle Wilson*. I kept it there because it cracked me up and it reminded me that Dad was once my age.

For a while tossing out shoes and jeans I'd outgrown kept me distracted, but then I quickly sank back into worrying. The afternoon dragged like a worm inching his way up the Eiffel Tower.

Outside it had started to rain again. Twig didn't have a jacket with her. The phone rang at six thirty, but it was Mom calling to tell us she was bringing home Mr. Pham's chicken pho for dinner.

After I hung up, I stared at the phone. *"Ring. Ring,"* I whispered. But it stayed silent. I walked over to the window. It was only a little drizzle. A few minutes later, a shot of lightning pierced the sky, followed by thunder.

I hurried downstairs, where Dad was filling glasses with ice cubes.

"Dad, I need to tell you something."

~

When I was finished filling him in, Dad told me to call Twig's mom. Just as I went to pick up the receiver, the phone rang.

Mrs. Wagner asked, "Rylee, is Twig there?"

I spilled my guts, telling her the plan and where I last saw Twig. Mr. Wagner had moved to Amarillo, so five minutes later, Dad and I picked up Twig's mom and headed down the old highway where, only a few hours before, Twig and I journeyed.

Inside the truck, Mrs. Wagner didn't bother to lower her rain jacket hood. It was as if she wanted to shut us out, or maybe just me.

Lightning cracked the gray sky while the rain poured down. The sun was hidden behind low clouds, but I could see the beams casting a golden haze on the horizon. It was as beautiful as a painting, and I might have stared at it longer, watching it set, if I hadn't been looking for Twig.

We passed the cowshed where we waited out the storm, talking about our futures, my safe, boring one and her grand, adventurous one. When we reached the steep twist in the road, I spotted Twig's bike. It was lying flat on the ground near the shoulder of the road like it had been abandoned in a hurry.

"Stop!" I hollered, pointing it out.

"Dear God," Mrs. Wagner uttered, and covered her mouth.

I was thinking the worst, too—struck by lightning, attacked by a coyote, picked up by some pervert. All the possibilities that made me turn around.

Dad parked on the shoulder, switched on his caution lights, and told us to stay in the truck.

My hand gripped the door handle, but I obeyed and stayed put. I stared at the floorboard, avoiding Mrs. Wagner, my heart thumping against my chest as Dad called Twig's name.

Mrs. Wagner jumped out of the truck and ran through the downpour frantically, crying out, "Twig!"

I should have told Dad when he first got home. Minutes could make a difference.

"She's not here," Dad hollered, motioning for Mrs. Wagner to head back with him to the truck.

Inside the truck, Dad's raincoat dripped on the seat. "That's a pretty steep climb," he said. "Cal bikes a lot, but I've only managed it myself once. She probably walked to the overlook from here."

Mrs. Wagner focused straight ahead as the windshield wipers swished back and forth.

Dad glanced over at her. "There's a shoulder along the road the whole way."

The road was empty except for us, but Dad kept his caution lights on and drove slowly up the incline. We looked from east to west and north to south, high and low as if she'd drop out of the sky.

We reached the overlook. Someone was sitting on top of a picnic table, huddled with her arms hugging her knees. The sun, now on the horizon, had broken through the clouds and cast a pinky orange on her. Her hair and clothes were drenched, and she was shaking. It was Twig.

She looked in our direction, and it seemed to take her a moment to realize who we were. When she did, she shifted her legs and turned away from us.

Mrs. Wagner got out of the truck. I started to follow her, but Dad stopped me. "Stay put, Rylee."

I leaned back and watched her mom rush toward her. Mrs. Wagner took off her raincoat and tried to slip it on Twig, but Twig pushed it away. Finally she reluctantly got off the table and followed Mrs. Wagner to the truck.

When Twig joined me in the back seat, I sent her a weak smile. She didn't say a word, just sat as close to the door as possible, pressing her cheek against the window while raindrops raced down the glass.

BOWL-A-RAMA CAFÉ

CHAPTER 12

I didn't try to call Twig all weekend. I thought about it, but what would I have said?

"You probably saved her life," Mom told me. "You have nothing to apologize about."

But why did it feel like I did? Why was *squim* the only word that I wished I could say to her?

Saying sorry was easy for me. Besides, even though telling was for a good reason, I had betrayed her.

~

Monday I waited by our lockers before school. I was starting to get good at rearranging mine. Language arts book on top. History and pre-algebra next. Then I reversed the order—pre-algebra, history, language arts. Then the spiral notebooks—red, yellow, green, and blue.

Juan Leon stopped by. "Did you lose something?"

"Not really," I said.

I must have really looked like a dork if Juan Leon came down to earth from Math Planet and noticed me shuffling through notebooks. The whole time I kept glancing back at the entrance, waiting for Twig. The first bell rang, and everyone made their way to their homerooms.

Except me.

Then she appeared, walking hand in hand toward the school with Vernon. They wore matching army jackets. When they entered the school, Vernon noticed me right off. He smirked my way and said, "Catch you later," to Twig, who moved slowly in my direction, avoiding my eyes.

She opened her locker, gathered her books, and started to walk away.

I called her name.

She stopped.

"Twig, I only told because I was afraid for you."

"You're always afraid," she said. "Afraid to do anything wrong. Go ahead and live your perfect little life."

I forgot how to breathe. The last bell rang, and I stayed leaning against the locker, watching her walk away, her long legs moving at a carefree pace toward her homeroom.

I was still there in the wide hallway by my locker, staring in at the trophy case glass, when I noticed Mr. Arlo's reflection behind me.

"Rylee, are you okay?" he gently asked.

"Yes." I snapped out of my daze. "Yes, sir."

"Better get to class." Then, as if he remembered he was the principal, his tone changed. "You're officially late. For the very first time, I might add."

∾

In history, the only class Twig and I had together, she settled at the back next to Vernon and never looked my way. At lunch she sat with him and his crony at what Twig had named the Jackass Table. She was laughing and twisting straws into animals like she used to do with me.

The whole day I felt like I was swimming through a fog. Nothing seemed clear. After school I picked up the phone several times to call Twig, but changed my mind.

Then Dad gave me some money and told me to go pick up burgers, since Mom was working late. I was relieved to have something to do.

~

At the Bowl-a-Rama, Ferris showed me the picture Miss Myrtie Mae left him of Dad and Uncle Cal as boys atop the café's roof.

"They thought I didn't know, but I always did," Ferris said. "Customers would tell me it sounded like I had giant squirrels scampering around up there."

By now I figured Dad didn't mean we needed to keep the picture a secret, so I told Ferris.

"Zachary Beaver? Yeah, I remember him. I baptized that boy in Gossimer Lake."

"You did?"

"Yeah, your dad and Cal were there. Malcolm Clifton, too."

"Really?" I wanted to ask more, but our order was ready and no one liked cold fries.

Before I made it out the door, Ferris said, "Zachary had a funny middle name, but for the life of me, I can't remember it."

As soon as I stepped out of the Bowl-a-Rama Café, I saw her. Twig was making her way down the square. She lowered her head when she noticed me and slowed her pace, but I kept moving toward her.

We reached each other in front of Earline's Real Estate office. Twig started to brush past me. "Wait, Twig," I said.

She froze, but focused on the concrete at her feet.

"Twig, why won't you forgive me?" My question sounded pathetic, and part of me hated myself for asking it, but I didn't know how to not be friends with her.

She lifted her head and glared at me. "What are you talking about?"

"About Friday."

"Friday was a long time ago." She stared in the window of Earline's office. Earline was typing at a desk, and her back was to us.

"What is it, then?" I asked.

Earline turned around, smiled, and waved. We both fake smiled and waved back as if we were still best friends who had just run into each other.

"What is it?" I repeated. "What did I do?"

Twig took a big breath, then let it out. Her voice softened. "Sometimes things change. Things you never think will change. Look what happened in New York."

"It's awful," I said. "It doesn't seem real."

"If you were at an airport when it happened, you'd know it was real."

I thought back to that night when Twig called me. She'd been so happy that I'd checked on her. How did everything drift so far from that moment?

Twig continued. "Then I get home and find out my parents are splitting up. I know my dad has a temper, but he's never laid a hand on Mom. She says what happened in New York made her think how short life was, and she doesn't want to spend it with my dad. She doesn't love him anymore."

I was the only one who could hear her, but it was as if she were saying the words to herself, trying to make sense of it all. I reached out and touched Twig's arm.

But she stepped back and tensed her jaw. "And you knew already, didn't you?"

"Yes," I said softly.

"Go live your perfect life. You don't need me. You have everything."

Then she moved along, leaving me standing alone. I stayed there a second, listening to the *tap, tap* of Earline's typewriter. I'd done everything I could do. I'd apologized, practically begged for forgiveness, but it was no use. Then I moved away, clutching the bag of burgers and fries, picking up my pace. My walk became a run as I hurried home, making a big promise to myself every step of the way—that I would never ever care about Twig Wagner again.

Original Soda Fountain Inside

CHAPTER 13

When she was alive, Miss Myrtie Mae's home had been Antler's best decorated house during the holidays. Even though Dad threw white lights on the bushes in front of our home every December, it wasn't anywhere near as spectacular. After every Thanksgiving, Miss Myrtie Mae hired Mr. Pham to hang lights from the rooflines of her house and gazebo, and twist string lights around her naked cottonwood's branches.

Miss Myrtie Mae was partial to blinking lights until Eb Gambert, who lived across the street, claimed he got epileptic seizures just by looking in his bathroom mirror.

Now the only festive thing on Miss Myrtie Mae's house was the gaudy wreath Miss Earline hung on the door, hoping to attract a potential buyer. She'd only had one showing since the sign went up, and she called those people tire kickers, a nosy couple from Clarendon who wanted to see inside the house but had no intention to buy it.

Since September I stopped walking by the house, because it reminded me of what had happened with Twig. Our friendship had once seemed so strong and unbreakable, but was now declining at such a rate it would never be the same.

I'd always thought there was no better place to live than Antler, but these days, I found myself wondering what it would be like to call somewhere else home. I daydreamed of living in Paris with Aunt Scarlett.

Mom didn't mention Twig anymore. In her opinion, I didn't deserve Twig's treatment. Dad, on the other hand, spoke as if our broken friendship was a temporary thing.

"Divorce is hard on kids," he added. "I know."

He was talking about Opa and Grandpa. I often forgot about them being married or divorced, probably because Grandpa had died before Opa returned to Antler. I don't ever remember seeing them together in the same room. It seemed one minute Grandpa was giving me horsey rides, and the next minute he was gone. Opa seemed to waltz into our lives right after that.

Dad said not to give up on Twig. He told me that even he and Uncle Cal went through a bad patch.

I wanted to ask, *How about Zachary Beaver?* Something must have not worked out with him.

Mom's *Les Misérables* poster still hadn't been framed, and Miss Myrtie Mae's photograph remained in the corner of our living room. Sometimes I pulled it away from the wall and stared into the boy's eyes, asking, "Where did you go, Zachary Beaver?"

On New Year's Day, I decided to go ahead and ask Dad, "Why don't you want to find him?"

"Rylee," he said, "to put it simply, 1971 was a tough summer, and Zachary's visit was the best part of it."

"That's what doesn't make sense. Seems like you'd want to find him, then."

Dad looked away to the picture in the corner. "He was a really big guy."

It was interesting to me how Dad didn't say the word that most people would use to describe Zachary.

"Your mom is right. He could be dead. There's a good chance of that. I want to remember him like he was that summer when the three of us became friends."

I thought of Twig and how, even though we weren't friends anymore, I hoped one day she'd remember how we'd shared some great times together. Then I silently promised myself I'd never ask Dad about Zachary Beaver again.

～

At the end of February the last winter snow thawed, and the date for the new library's groundbreaking was announced. It would be held the first Saturday in April. The day after the announcement, there wasn't a cloud in the sky, and the sun shone so bright it lifted my spirits. I hadn't ridden since last summer, so I dragged my bike out and went around town, pedaling past places Twig and I used to visit. After being cooped up indoors for weeks, it felt good to be outside with the sunshine warming my back and the crisp air chilling my face.

Mr. Pham was making his way down my street, and he tipped his green fedora at me when I passed by. He walked every morning, no matter the weather, always wearing his finest clothes. That day he had on a trench coat and a plaid scarf around his neck. As usual, he carried two bags, one for litter and the other for soda cans. Ferris said he'd turned them in to the recycling plant for years and that there was no telling how much money he had.

I moved along the streets of Antler, trying to push away any memory I had about the days Twig and I rode together. I avoided Allsup's, but decided to make the corner onto Miss Myrtie Mae's street. When I passed her house, I could tell something was different. It took a moment before I realized the sign was missing. Either a Jerk had taken it as a prank or someone had bought Miss Myrtie Mae's house. By sundown, we learned that it was neither. The new owner from Brooklyn had decided to move to Antler.

CHAPTER 14

The Toscani family was due to move into Miss Myrtie Mae's old house during spring break. Their last name was all we knew about them, but everyone figured they must have kids since they chose that week.

Spring break week also meant Mom, Dad, and I would take turns at the snow cone stand. Usually I hated having to spend my break working because that robbed me of time hanging out with Twig, but now I looked forward to it. Selling snow cones would give me something to do.

That first morning, I started for my shift and saw an unfamiliar burgundy SUV with a Vermont license plate easing down our street. Twig and I could finally cross Vermont off our list. But what would she care now? It was a dumb game anyway.

When the SUV turned at our corner onto Cottonwood Street, pulling into Miss Myrtie Mae's driveway, I realized the car must belong to the Toscanis. Before I took off for the stand, I told Mom that I thought the new neighbors had arrived.

Mayzee slid down the banister. "I want to see them!"

She'd been told a million times not to do that, but never got into real trouble.

"Mayzee Wilson," Mom said, "what did I tell you, young lady?" She turned back to me. "I'll make a carrot cake for them. Don't worry, I'll make one for us, too."

Mom's carrot cake was her specialty. Double cream cheese frosting, cake so moist it melted in your mouth. No one knew the recipe. Ferris had begged to have it for years. After the hundredth time that he asked and she declined, he took a stab at it.

When Mom tasted his attempt, she told him, "Nope, that's not it."

"Yeah," Ferris said, "I reckoned that."

He even promised to put her name on the menu if she'd give the recipe to him. "I'll call it Tara Wilson's 24k Carrot Cake."

"Nope," Mom had told him. "That recipe's going with me to the grave. How do you think I got my husband? That cake is guaranteed man bait."

If another year went by without getting my first kiss, I might need that recipe. Although I was pretty sure the cake didn't have anything to do with Mom plucking Dad's heartstrings. The story I'd been told was that Mom had been crazy for Dad most of her life, but she was seven years younger and he'd never paid much attention to her.

They only lived a few blocks apart, and would see each other often around town. But years later they bumped into each other at the Dallas–Fort Worth Airport. Dad was traveling home from a history teachers' conference, and Mom had celebrated graduating from college by visiting Aunt Scarlett, who was living in New York at the time. When Mom spotted Dad at the

departure gate, she plopped herself next to him, starting a conversation. Because of bad weather, their flight
time to Amarillo kept being postponed. They waited
it out, making their way around the airport, eating
nachos for dinner, drinking coffee later, and sharing an
ice cream sundae.

Their flight was officially canceled at midnight, and
they were rescheduled the next morning. When the
airlines brought out cots for the passengers, Mom and
Dad put theirs side by side.

Dad insisted he didn't get a wink of sleep because
he wanted to make sure Mom's purse and bag didn't
get stolen, but Mom claimed she didn't dare blink the
entire night, staring at Dad as he slept, thinking how
lucky she was to have spent an entire day with Toby
Wilson. They were married three months later. That
may not sound like a fairy tale to most people, but to
me, it was pretty romantic.

~

Before I left for the stand, I told Mayzee to find out if someone my age had moved into Miss Myrtie Mae's house.

She was stretched out on the couch, flat on her back, reading a picture book, holding it high above her head. "It will cost you," she said, not bothering to glance over at me.

Her piggy bank was for only one thing—a trip to Disney World. She was determined to get there, one nickel at a time.

"I'll pay you fifty cents," I told her.

"No deal!" She raised her legs to the ceiling, flexing her feet.

"Okay, a dollar."

Mayzee dropped the book. "Deal!"

∼

By the time the ice machine was turned on and the OPEN sign was facing out, I had my first customer. It was Vernon. Before he and Twig started hanging out, he hardly combed his hair. Now he heaped on so much product that in a gust of wind, his hair flapped, saluting.

"Medium Lemon Tang," he said, "and an extra-large Bahama Mama."

He didn't have to tell me who wanted the Lemon

Tang. I glanced around for Twig, but she was nowhere in sight.

I pulled two cups from the stack.

Vernon smirked. "So have you heard, those New Yorkers are moving in today?"

I started to nod, then changed my mind. Maybe he knew more about them. Trying not to sound interested, I said, "Really?"

"Yep. Heard it's a mom and her son," he said.

I gave him a deadpan stare and handed him his Bahama Mama snow cone with such a skimpy amount of syrup it looked pink. He must have noticed because he pushed it back at me. "A little extra, like how you made hers."

I drenched it with the red syrup and when he asked how much he owed, I added in a dollar.

"Did your prices go up?"

"For the extra syrup. It's not free."

Our menu board confirmed the additional costs, but we never enforced it. Until now.

He dug in his pocket and threw the dollar bills on the counter. I hated when people did that, like you weren't good enough for them to place the money in your hand. Then like a big shot, he dropped a quarter into the tip jar.

I watched him leave to see if I could spot Twig's hiding place, but he left the square and slipped around the corner.

The afternoon dragged, with hardly any customers. I was disappointed because I wanted to learn more about the Toscanis. A train passed by with its *ka-nunk, ka-nunk, ka-nunk*. Not a single car traveling down 287 stopped at the stand. We didn't get that many out-of-towners anyway. Most of them stopped at Allsup's. To make time pass, I wiped down all the syrup bottles, turned the radio up, and sang "Survivor" with Destiny's Child. The radio played the song so often I was sick of it, but I sang anyway, adding in a side shuffle with shoulder action.

Then a *tap, tap, tap* interrupted me.

I swung around. The bottle slipped from my hands and broke on the asphalt.

"Sorry," the guy at the counter said. "I didn't mean to scare you."

He appeared to be about my age. His dark hair was cut close to his head, except for a tiny braid touching the back of his collar.

"You didn't." I glanced down. Blueberry syrup spread at my feet. "How long were you standing there?"

"Not long." He grinned. He'd heard.

"Nice song," he said.

My face burned.

"What flavor broke?" His voice was different—raspy, with no Panhandle twang.

"Blueberry." I started to pick up the pieces. It was a clean break, three pieces in a puddle of dark purple. Carefully, I picked up the glass and dropped it in the garbage can, and wiped off my hands with a wet rag. "What can I get you? We have everything except Cotton Candy today."

"And Blueberry," he added.

"What?" I looked down at the purple splatters on my shirt. My face was a furnace running full blast.

"Right. We're out of Cotton Candy and Blueberry." My voice came out deep and formal. "We have some new flavors, too. Honey Pickle Juice and Burnt Marshmallow."

He scowled. "I'll pass on those."

I glanced around for his car, but he was too young to drive. Where had he come from?

He leaned over the counter and read the new board silently.

"What is a Bahama Mama?" He had an unusual accent.

That stupid tickle in my throat showed up, and after four *er-ums*, I began to explain in a high-pitched voice I didn't recognize. Instead of just listing the ingredients, I told him the entire story of our business, how there used to be a snow cone stand here owned by Wylie Womack, known for its Bahama Mama snow cones, how my family bought a stand since my parents were teachers and it was our whole family's side business now.

I couldn't stop talking.

He smiled, and when I finally shut up, he said, "I'll have the house special."

"What's that?" I asked.

"The Bahama Mama?" he said slowly.

"Oh, of course."

"Make it a large."

"You bet."

While I waited for the ice to drop into the cup, he remained quiet and gazed around, past the square, looking toward the highway.

I poured the regular amount of syrup. Then I added a little more.

"What's down the road?" He tilted his head west.

"Amarillo," I said, handing him his snow cone.

"Nowhere, huh?"

I didn't know what to say to that. To us, Amarillo was the big city.

He paid me, but before he walked away, he asked, "Is your little sister Mayzee?"

"Yes." I knew exactly where he came from.

He punched his spoon through the ice. "She said you owe her a dollar."

CHAPTER 15

The Toscanis had been in Antler two days, and that was
all Antler wanted to talk about. People asked the same
things that most everyone else wanted to know:

Why did their license plate say Vermont and not
New York?

Would Mrs. Toscani's husband be joining them?

And then what everyone wanted to know most:

Why did they move to Antler?

According to Mom, Maria Toscani seemed surprised

when she gave her a cake a couple of hours after they moved in. Mom also shared her Tara's Rules of Antler Survival. She told Mrs. Toscani about Peggy Cartwright's gym barn and the Bronze Baby Tanning Salon on the square. She advised her to skip Bambi's Cut and Curl and make her hair appointments in Amarillo or she'd have a bad hair day that would last an entire season. She told her that the Wag-a-Bag grocery store had the best peaches brought in from Hedley, but she'd have to forget about finding a decent avocado there.

Mom said she asked Mrs. Toscani about the Vermont license plate, since we thought they were moving here from New York. Mrs. Toscani told her that her cousin from Bennington sold his car to her.

"What's her son's name?" I asked.

"I don't think she told me," Mom said. "She was a little preoccupied because the moving van had arrived."

After riding to the post office to mail a bill for Dad, I stopped by the Bowl-a-Rama Café for a vanilla shake.

Inside, Ferris was wiping down a table. "Have you met the Toscanis yet?"

"Sort of," I told him. "The son came by our stand,

I think." I didn't know why I was acting like he could have been someone else, but we really hadn't officially met.

"They ordered hamburgers earlier," he said.

"Two with everything," Mr. Pham added, "including mayonnaise."

It was kind of a sin to eat hamburgers with mayo in Texas. Mustard was perfectly fine, but you didn't want to ruin the taste of good beef with the greasy stuff. I didn't even know what mayonnaise was until I was five and Mom made egg salad from all the leftover Easter eggs.

Ferris limped to the kitchen and wrung out the dishcloth at the sink. "Yep, I guess it's just the boy and his mama. Seems like a nice kid, but it was all I could do to not grab the scissors and cut off that itty-bitty braid."

"What's his name?" I asked.

Ferris studied me a long second, and his mouth spread into a giant toothy grin. "Now, why would you want to know that?"

All at once, I felt like my feet were on fire, and the

heat spread up my body and didn't stop until it reached the tip of my head.

"Rylee, it's refreshing to see a girl blush these days." Ferris winked.

"His name is Joe," Mr. Pham shouted from the kitchen. I was so thankful no other customers were there.

"That's right," Ferris said. "Joe Toscani. Does that sound sweet to your ears, Rylee?"

"Don't listen to Ferris." Mr. Pham placed the milkshake on the counter. "He makes trouble."

∼

When I reached the snow cone stand, Mom was waiting on Miss Earline and her niece. After they left, she told me to ask our new neighbors over for dinner the next night.

"Don't you want to ask them?" I wasn't looking forward to seeing Joe again anytime soon. Maybe I'd feel differently in a few weeks when he forgot about my song-and-dance routine.

"I've met them," Mom said. "Now, go over and

introduce yourself and ask them to come for lasagna tomorrow night."

"Okay," I muttered. At least dinner was going to be lasagna. Hard to mess up a frozen meal. Mom's desserts could win first place in any baking contest, but one taste of her plain ol' cooking would cause a mouse to return every crumb and choose to starve. Her roast beef was tough as jerky, and her watery mashed potatoes dripped off the fork.

When I started to leave, Mom said, "The son is cute. I think he might be about your age."

My stomach hurt, replaying the whole Destiny's Child/ blueberry syrup incident. Plus I suspected Mayzee told him why I owed her a dollar. But I followed Mom's orders and pedaled slowly toward Miss Myrtie Mae's house.

A couple of empty boxes were on the corner of their lawn. I guess they didn't know about the dumpster in the alley behind their house yet.

By the time I reached the door, it opened without me having a chance to knock or ring the doorbell. Joe walked out and almost bumped into me.

"Oh," he said. "Hello, again."

"Hi," I said.

Joe stepped back and pushed the door open wider. Stacks of moving boxes were behind him. "Did you get blueberry syrup back in?"

"What? Oh, no. That's not why I'm here. My mom wanted me to come over and ask you and your mom to dinner tomorrow night."

He leaned against the doorway. *"Who's* asking?"

"My mom."

"But *you're* asking." He smirked.

"I'm asking technically, but my mom asked me to ask you."

"So *who's* asking?"

I looked at him, confused.

"My mom is Tara Wilson."

"But *who's* asking?"

I froze.

"I'm Joe," he said. "What's your name?"

"Oh, I'm sorry. I get it now. I'm Rylee. Rylee Wilson." I held out my hand for a shake.

Instead, he slapped my hand like he was giving me a sideways five. Then he turned, facing the giant foyer. "Mom, Rylee Wilson is at the door for you."

"Who?" she yelled from the back of the house.

He faced me again. "Is your mom a good cook?"

"Not really," I said.

"Wow, what a way to welcome us to Nowhere, Texas. Invite us over for a bad meal."

"She's a good baker. She made the carrot cake."

"That is good. Actually, great. Her dinner couldn't be all that bad."

At least she hadn't messed up heating frozen lasagna. Well, once she did leave a pan of it in the oven too long because she got caught up watching the Oscars. The noodles were a bit rubbery, but edible.

Joe's mom was at the door now. Her dark hair was twisted in a messy bun, and even with no makeup, she was pretty. "Hi," she said.

"Hi. My mom is Tara Wilson. I think you met her a couple of days ago."

"And you are?" Joe reminded me.

"I'm sorry. I'm Rylee. Rylee Wilson." I held out my hand, and we shook.

"Nice to meet you, Rylee. I'm Maria Toscani. That was thoughtful of your mom to bring over a cake. It was delicious."

"Tara's mom wants us to come over for dinner tomorrow night," Joe told her, "but Rylee says her mom's a bad cook."

Mrs. Toscani laughed. "That couldn't be true."

My face felt hot. I didn't know what to say next.

"Please tell your mom we'd love to come," Mrs. Toscani said. "Can we bring anything?"

I wanted to ask, *Could you leave your son at home?* Instead I said, "No thank you. Mom has it all taken care of."

CHAPTER 16

Lasagna Night turned into Meatloaf Night because Mom said it would be awful to serve our new neighbors a warmed frozen meal the first time she asked them over.

"Not so awful," I told her.

"They'll think I don't know how to cook." She tied on her apron that read SHRIMP, Dad's pet name for her.

"Your dad is going to grill endive, but why don't you make a salad?" Mom asked me. "You can never have too many vegetables."

"Okay, but are you sure you don't want to serve lasagna?" I asked. "It would be easier."

"Oh, I can do this in my sleep." She pulled the ground beef from the freezer and stuck it in the microwave, disregarding the defrost button and pressing the cook time on seven minutes. How could someone who measured every speck of flour and sugar when she baked a cake be so careless about cooking meat?

The last time we ate her meatloaf, Aunt Scarlett was visiting. She sawed her crisp dinner into tiny bites, using a butter knife. Instead of eating, she scooted the pieces around her plate and drank four glasses of water during the meal.

Even though I remembered Mr. Pham telling me about their hamburger order, I asked, "What if the Toscanis are vegetarians?"

"Rylee, they're Italian."

"What's that got to do with it?"

She looked at me like I said Neil Armstrong didn't walk on the moon. "Veal Parmesan? Spaghetti and meatballs? Pepperoni pizza?"

"They're Italian *American*, Mom. Anyway that doesn't mean they always eat Italian food or meat."

"Rylee, you're acting as if you don't like my meatloaf."

"Oh, Mom!" Saying that had gotten me out of a lot of sticky conversations with her.

"Can I put cheddar in the salad?" I asked.

"Sure." Mom checked on the ground beef, stabbing a fork through it. Part of the meat was cooked, but when she discovered that it wasn't thawed all the way, she zapped it on high for two more minutes.

I rinsed the lettuce and put it in the spinner to dry. Then I gathered the tomatoes, carrots, and olives.

The microwave stopped buzzing, and Mom pulled out the meat. It was as gray as an old barn owl. She dumped it into the glass bowl and cracked two eggs.

"Oops," she said. She'd accidentally dropped half of a shell into the meatloaf. Squinting, she used a spoon to try and scoop up the shell bits. She gave up, resting the spoon in the sink. "Oh, well. Good fiber."

∼

By six o'clock, the smell of burnt onions overwhelmed the house. At 6:01, the doorbell rang. At 6:02, the Toscanis' wrinkled noses had clearly picked up the kitchen catastrophe.

Maria Toscani wore a navy sundress with a wide ivory belt emphasizing her tiny waist. She had the same coloring as Joe—olive skin, thick dark hair, and brown eyes. I checked out Joe's eyes. He had the longest eyelashes.

Mom, Mayzee, and I were greeting them at the door when Uncle Cal showed up. He immediately noticed Maria and pulled off his baseball cap, running his fingers through the small amount of hair he had remaining.

"Cal," Mom said, "this is Maria Toscani and her son. Our new neighbors."

He nodded, and his cheeks turned a little pink. Uncle Cal and I could have had a blushing contest.

Maria smiled, offering her hand. "Nice to meet you, Cal."

Uncle Cal held Maria's hand and stared at it like he wanted to plant a kiss on her fingers. When he was still holding it a moment later, Maria pulled her hand back.

"Oh," Uncle Cal said like he'd just realized she'd only wanted to shake. Then he held out his hand to

Joe, who turned away and moseyed over to the living area.

Dad entered from the back door. "Hello! I'm glad you could make it. I'm Toby."

Maria held her hand out to Dad. He wasn't like Uncle Cal. He knew what to do and shook.

"Maria Toscani. Thanks for having us over. That's my son, Joe."

Dad crossed the room where Joe was standing directly in front of the Zachary photograph. Joe reluctantly took Dad's outstretched hand, but dropped it quickly.

Dad raised his eyebrows, then said, "I'm grilling endive outside, Joe—you want to join me? Cal?"

Uncle Cal went, but Joe said, "I'll stay here."

"Thank you for asking him," Maria quickly added.

Mom invited Maria to follow her into the kitchen while she finished up. That left me alone with Joe, because Mayzee had disappeared for some reason. The only time I desperately needed her to bug me, and she'd deserted ship.

Joe pulled the Zachary picture away from the corner and peeked on the other side.

"You can flip it around and look at it, if you want," I told him.

He did, studying it for a long while. He was clearly interested, so interested that it made me remember how Twig had seemed bored when I told her about Zachary.

Finally Joe spoke. "My uncle's a big guy, too. Are you related to this guy?"

"Zachary Beaver? No, he's an old friend of my dad and Uncle Cal's." I explained how Miss Myrtie Mae left him the photo in her will.

"Did he live in Nowhere, Texas, too?"

A prickle ran up my arm. "No, he didn't, and believe it or not, Antler is included on the Texas map."

"You sound like the Ambassador. The Ambassador of Nowhere, Texas."

I took a breath, reminding myself that he was a guest, trying to avoid those brown eyes and long eyelashes.

He went back to studying the photo. "She wasn't a bad photographer."

"I know. She was good. I never saw her take a picture, but Dad says she used to do it all the time. She was really old when I was born, but I went to her house a lot."

"You mean *our* house?"

"Well—" I cleared my throat. "Yes. Dad used to mow her . . . I mean *your* lawn."

"Does he still want to?" Joe asked.

"What?"

He half laughed. "You really don't have a sense of humor, do you?"

"Yes, I do," I snapped.

Joe backed away, palms up. "Okay, I take it back."

I didn't know if he was trying to be funny or insulting. It kind of seemed like both.

He eased the photo back to its leaning position on the wall, and for a long moment, neither of us spoke.

I felt trapped.

Mayzee was setting the table, something she actually thought was fun.

"I'll help you," I called out from the living area.

"No! It's *my* turn." She rolled a napkin and tied it in a snug knot.

I was so relieved when Mom called out, "Time for dinner!"

"Warning," I said in a low voice. "Mom's meatloaf may be on the rubbery side. Your gut might bounce back to New York."

Joe broke into a quick grin. "Maybe you're right. Maybe you do have a sense of humor."

Welcome to
ANTLER
IF YOU DON'T WANT SOMETHING TOLD,
DON'T TELL US!
POPULATION 856   ELEVATION 3,600

CHAPTER 17

Somewhere between the dry meatloaf and Mom's delicious blackberry cobbler, we learned that Maria Toscani was a physician's assistant and that she'd start looking for a job in Amarillo as soon as they got settled. Both of her parents had died a while back, she told us.

"It's only Joe and me," she said.

Joe, who had been quiet through the entire meal, spoke up. "How about Uncle Tony? And Aunt Marissa? And Tasha and Sal? They're family, aren't they?"

Mrs. Toscani gave him a sharp look. "Of course."

The room grew quiet except for the scraping sounds of forks moving bites of meatloaf around. Mayzee sneakily dragged half of hers across the plate and hid it under her salad.

"What neighborhood in Brooklyn?" Dad asked.

"The best one," Joe said.

Mrs. Toscani spoke up. "Bay Ridge. It's in South Brooklyn."

"Cal has a sister in Park Slope," Dad said.

"Oh?" Mrs. Toscani smiled politely at Uncle Cal.

"She's a theater costume designer." Uncle Cal's gaze was fixed only on Mrs. Toscani. "Mom and Dad tried to get her to come home after what happened in September, but she wouldn't."

Mrs. Toscani glanced down at her watch.

"Maybe she is home," Joe said. "Some people don't run away."

Mrs. Toscani looked out our kitchen window.

"That was so terrible what happened," Mom said. "September eleventh still doesn't seem real."

Both Joe and Mrs. Toscani popped bites of Mom's

meatloaf in their mouths and chewed, chewed, chewed.

After the Toscanis left, Uncle Cal settled on a bar stool and watched us clean the kitchen. Mom and Dad started clearing the table while I filled the sink up with soapy water.

"Did Joe tell you anything about his dad?" Mom asked me.

I shook my head, feeling bad that I hadn't given it much thought.

Before dropping the pan into water, Mom dug out the remaining meatloaf and placed it in a storage container. I almost groaned.

"She never mentioned if she was divorced or widowed," Mom said.

"Well, the circumstances don't matter," said Uncle Cal. "She's not married, and that's a beautiful thing. She's a beautiful thing."

Mom sighed. "Oh, Cal, are you falling in love again?"

Dad placed his hand firmly on Uncle Cal's bony shoulder. "Okay, Romeo, remember, she's our neighbor. When the romance is over, she's still our neighbor."

In bed, I remembered what Joe said about Kate probably thinking of New York as home. Maybe that was the way Joe felt too. That Bay Ridge was where he belonged. The same way I felt about Antler. I wondered if he'd ever give our town a chance.

He had called me the Ambassador of Nowhere. Didn't ambassadors represent the places where they were from? Maybe if I showed him what I loved most about our town—the Bowl-a-Rama Café, Opalina's Opry House, Innis's Drug Store's soda fountain bar, Gossimer Pit, where there used to be a lake, and Mrs. McKnight's rose tunnel—maybe then he would see that Antler was somewhere. My neck and face burned when I remembered what I'd always dreamed would happen under those salmon-colored petals. Well, maybe we would skip the rose tunnel.

CHAPTER 18

It was early morning, still dark outside, and I was wide awake. Outside my window the sound of a fast bicycle whirred past our house. Without looking, I knew it was Uncle Cal.

The morning could be lonesome for people like me, who rose before the alarm while the rest of the world slept. It was like arriving at a party too soon. I closed my eyes and thought about the day I'd planned.

By the time the sun came up, I heard Dad downstairs

moving around in the kitchen. We were expecting a syrup shipment, so a little later he left to meet the delivery guy at the stand. Dad would stay and work the morning shift.

Then I'd take his place at noon, since Mom would be with Mayzee at rehearsal for tomorrow night's presentation at the opry. Mayzee went on before the Polka Pals, a group from outside of Houston. On polka nights the audience looked like a sea of silver and gray, stomping their feet to the accordion music. Polka night wasn't my favorite.

I ate quickly and washed up. It was going to be unusually hot today, so I wove my hair in a long braid. Then I unbraided it. I tried a deep part and swept my hair across, covering my left eye. Nope. Next I tried to imagine myself with a pixie hairdo like Twig's. Not a chance. It would look like a knit cap tightly hugging my head. Besides Twig seemed to be growing hers out. Finally I gave up and gathered it into a high ponytail.

Mom had skipped the gym and was still sleeping. It was eight o'clock. Joe was probably asleep, too. I decided to check for early morning movement anyway, dragging my bike out of the garage and riding around the corner to Miss Myrtie Mae's house.

To my surprise, Joe was sitting sideways on the deep second-floor windowsill of Miss Myrtie Mae's old bedroom, the one she slept in before moving to a room downstairs. I remembered her staring out of the window on the first floor a lot the last year of her life, her pale face against the sheer drapes. Twig had said she looked like a ghost, peering out on the world.

Joe wore sweatpants and a white T-shirt, and his feet were bare. When he noticed me, he called down, "Hello, Ambassador."

"How about a tour?" I asked.

He shrugged. "Nothing else to do."

"Get your bike," I told him.

"I don't have one." He said it quickly and with a matter-of-fact tone, as if he didn't have any plans to ever own a bike. I'd never known anyone my age who didn't have one. Although I might as well not have had one now. I hadn't ridden mine much since Twig and I stopped being friends.

"We can walk," I told him. "Wanna meet over at my house after you dress?"

"And eat my Wheaties. They'll make me good and strong." He flexed his skinny arm.

About fifteen minutes later, he was at my front porch.

Next door, Mrs. McKnight was in her garden, spreading compost around her rose plants. The leaves had started to appear, and they'd be blooming in a month or two. I waved to her, and she waved back. "That's Uncle Cal's mom. Come on, I'll introduce you."

I stepped in her direction, but Joe grabbed my wrist. "Actually, I really don't feel like meeting anyone."

"Oh. Okay." I kept walking down our road.

After we passed a few houses, Joe asked, "So she's your grandmother?"

"Who?" Then I realized he meant Mrs. McKnight. "No, we're not related."

"I don't get it. I thought Cal was your uncle."

"We call him that because he and my dad have been best friends all their lives."

"And the guy in the picture?"

"You mean Zachary?"

"Yeah, didn't you say he was their friend?"

"Yes, but he was only here a little while, a summer back in the 1970s."

"Where is he now?"

"I don't know."

"Is he alive?" Joe seemed as curious as me about Zachary.

I shrugged.

"Your dad doesn't know if he's alive?"

"No, he lost touch with him."

"Some friends," he muttered.

"You don't get it," I said, ticked now that he had insulted my dad and Uncle Cal. "Zachary was passing through town. He was here only a short time. People don't always stay in touch."

Joe stopped walking. "I don't believe that. If you're a true friend, you're a friend for life."

I was tired of being polite. "So are you going to stay in touch with your Brooklyn friends? And are they going to stay in touch with you?"

"Yeah, but I don't call everyone a friend. I have one

true friend. One person who knows me better than anyone. He knows what it's like when things aren't great, when things are the worst. And yeah, we're still friends. I talked to him last night on the phone."

"Well, you're lucky, then," I said in a soft voice. And I meant it.

The wind picked up so hard that Joe's braid wagged like a kite's tail.

"This stupid wind!" Joe says. "When does it stop?"

Never. The Panhandle wind was a pain, but he was as prickly as a cactus.

"And what's that stink?"

I sniffed the air. "What stink?"

"It smells like manure."

"That's the Martins' cattle feedlot." I hardly noticed because I'd grown up smelling it. "It's twelve miles away. You only smell it when the wind blows in a certain direction."

"All the time?"

I ignored his comment and kept moving.

Mr. and Mrs. Bastrop were sitting on their porch, drinking their coffee. I waved, but I didn't speak. They would have surely asked us to come over, and I didn't want to be rude.

For a while, we walked along in silence. Then the putter of Buster's family's blue pickup truck interrupted the quiet. When they got closer, they waved, and I greeted them, waving back. Buster, who has Down syndrome, opened his window and hollered, "Hey, Ry-lee! Go, Mustangs!"

I raised my fist in the air, and he did the same.

"Buster is our school teams' biggest fan," I explained.

Joe seemed baffled. "You know everyone here, huh?"

I nodded, thinking what he'd said a few moments ago; I'd always thought of them as friends. Now I was wondering, *Who is a friend?* If any of my neighbors moved away, would we stay in touch? Kate did, but she stayed in touch with everyone, sending birthday and Christmas cards to practically every citizen of Antler. But if Twig moved away, she probably wouldn't stay in touch. I was certain of that now. I hated the way our former friendship always wove its way into my thoughts.

We reached the square, but I didn't turn right. "We'll pick the square up on the way back," I told him.

At the feed store, a gigantic flag hung from the roof-line, spreading across the entire width of the porch.

"Wow," Joe said, sarcastically. "Patriotic."

"Mr. Garrett has kept the flag up since September eleventh. Want to go in?"

"No," he said firmly. "You see one feed store, you've seen them all."

"You have feed stores in Brooklyn?"

He scowled. "I don't want to go inside. Okay?"

"Whatever you say."

The parking lot had about twenty Ford and Chevy pickups.

As we passed the lot, Joe asked, "Do you have to own a pickup to live in Texas?"

It was a fair question, because there were a lot of pickup trucks in Antler.

"Well, most of their customers own farms or ranches."

Not far down the road was the nursing home, where a couple of workers were sitting on porch rockers, smoking cigarettes.

Next to the nursing home was the Antler Cemetery.

An old windmill in the center *click-clank*ed as its blades blurred against the cloudless sky. Joe turned away with such a force that I figured something must be wrong. Maybe his dad *was* dead. Or maybe he was thinking about his grandparents. Mrs. Toscani had said they'd been dead a few years. I don't know why I walked all the way to the edge of town. Nursing homes and cemeteries. He was probably realizing I wasn't the cool kid in school.

"Well, that's the east part of Antler," I said, heading back west.

We made our way around the square, and I named off the shops—Earline's Real Estate, Charlotte's Antiques, York's Hardware.

"I know how to read," Joe said.

Of course he did, but how could I give a tour when I couldn't introduce him to anybody? How could he understand what it was like to pass house after house, business after business, and know everyone under every roof? It was then I realized why Antler was so special to me. My feelings had nothing to do with brick and mortar, but everything to do with the people.

We approached the Bowl-a-Rama Café, and as always could be predicted, we found Ferris sitting outside.

"Oh no, not this guy," Joe mumbled.

"Hey, Rylee!" Ferris called out. "I see you've met my new friend, Joe."

Ignoring Joe's earlier request, I left him at the sidewalk and stepped toward Ferris.

His uncombed froth of gray hair made him look like a mad professor. Motioning with his arm, Ferris called out, "Step on up, Joe."

Reluctantly, Joe moved toward the porch.

"How would you like a job, Joe?" Ferris asked.

Joe crossed his arms in front of his chest. "Doing what?"

"Setting bowling pins. It's only two lanes. And you don't have to work every day, only when we open the lanes twice a week, at the most, once for the bowling clubs and another day for the public."

Joe smirked. "You don't have a machine that sets the pins?"

"What would be the fun in that?" Ferris said. "It's

ninepin bowling. The rules are a little different than regular bowling."

For years, two of Ferris's lanes had been broken. Then while visiting another bowling alley in the Texas hill country, he learned about ninepin bowling, where kids set the pins instead of machines. He decided what the heck? He'd save some money and have a new draw for an old sport.

"Ninepin?" Joe asked.

"That's right," Ferris said. "It's older than tenpin. Rylee knows all about it. She used to be our star."

My neck felt hot and sweaty. "Ferris exaggerates. I played when I was a kid."

"Yeah, she was so much younger. When was that? About a year or two ago?" Ferris winked at me.

I didn't know about being the star, but I'd been our team's highest scorer. I used to love it. But Twig was right. What was the point? Getting a big ugly trophy that no one would want to display?

"Think about it," Ferris told Joe. "You can take a look right now at the lanes."

Joe didn't answer. I couldn't help but wonder if he

was just rude or if everyone acted like that in New York. But Mrs. Toscani seemed nice.

"You don't have to give me an answer now," Ferris said. "Why don't you drop by this afternoon, after the lunch crowd, and then Vernon can demonstrate how to set the pins."

Joe sort of nodded.

Mr. Pham came in from his daily walk and tipped his green fedora at us.

"Good morning," he said.

"Morning, Mr. Pham," I said.

He could be awarded the prize for best-dressed man in Antler. Inside the café, he hung up his plaid sports coat and pulled off his hat and wing-tipped shoes. Then he tied on his apron and slipped on a worn pair of loafers.

"I might stop by later to talk more about the job," Joe said, not bothering to thank Ferris.

That was our cue to leave. "See you, Ferris," I said. "Bye, Mr. Pham. Have a good day."

Ferris seemed unfazed by Joe's rudeness. "Stay out of trouble, outlaws."

As soon as we were a few feet away, Joe asked, "What does Ferris do all day? Sit on the bread box and yap?"

"He's not lazy. For years he was the only cook."

I could see Joe wasn't that convinced, so I added, "And he has a war injury." I didn't tell him what Dad told me about Ferris shooting himself in the foot to keep from going to the Vietnam War. Even so, that still kind of made it a war injury.

Joe and I finished circling the square, passing our snow cone stand, where Dad was too busy to notice us. He was waiting on a family that I didn't recognize, probably people passing through town.

Sometimes travelers stopped and asked us all kinds of things about the history of Antler or how many people lived here. Dad thrived on that stuff. He recommended they stop down the road in Goodnight to see the famous rancher Charlie Goodnight's grave and tie a bandanna on the fence in front of it, or drive to the overlook to see the Palo Duro Canyon. Some out-of-towners wanted to know where Juan Garcia grew up. Dad would point across the railroad tracks, or if no other customers were waiting, he'd draw a little map on a scrap of paper. The people always thanked Dad and acted like they planned to take him up on his suggestions. Those were Dad's kind of people.

Those weren't Mom's kind of people. She dreaded those questions. When they asked her about Antler, she just smiled and said, "Oh, we're like any little Texas Panhandle town." They never asked her for more details, so maybe they really didn't want to know all the things Dad told them.

Joe and I finished our lap around the square, and I pointed out the drugstore across the way. "That's Innis's Drug Store."

Joe sighed. "I can read. Remember?"

I didn't care how cute he was. He was definitely rude.

We crossed the street, and Joe read the sign above the drugstore door. "'Original Soda Fountain Inside.' How cool. Oh, man, do they have egg creams?"

"Eggs and cream?" I asked him.

"No," he said. "You've never had an egg cream?"

"Nope—so is it a dessert with eggs and cream in it?"

"No eggs. No cream. Just milk, seltzer, and chocolate

syrup. When I was little, my uncle would take my cousins and me to Hinsch's every Saturday." He spread his arms wide and turned around. "Oh, man. If I could have one right now."

"Sorry, but we do have milkshakes."

"Nah." He was clearly disappointed.

We walked a few steps. The big window on the side gave a wide view of the fountain bar. Right off, I noticed Vernon and Twig sitting there, sipping milkshakes.

Joe noticed them too. "Who's that?"

"Him? Vernon. He's the pinsetter who works for Ferris."

"I mean *her*. Who is she?" He was clearly interested. What guy wouldn't be? Twig oozed confidence. Even the way she sat tall on her stool as she stirred her straw in her shake looked sophisticated.

"Twig Wagner."

And as we walked away, he twisted his head in her direction.

I picked up my pace so that when he finally awoke from Twig's spell, he had to sprint to catch up.

"Is something wrong?" he asked.

"Nope," I said.

He shrugged.

A little farther down Main Street was Opalina's Opry House. Even though he didn't want to meet anyone, no way would I pass the opry house and not stop and say hello to Opa.

"'Opalina's Opry House'?" Joe read aloud, then snorted. "I feel like I'm on another planet."

"That's my grandmother," I snapped. "She's a successful businesswoman. She's even recorded an album." I made her sound like she was Reba McEntire, even though none of Opa's songs had ever played on the radio.

Joe stared down. "I'm sorry," he muttered. "It's just very different here. I've never seen an opry house."

I changed my mind about dropping in on Opa.

We were quiet as we walked toward Allsup's, the last stop on the tour. No reason to take him to Gossimer Pit, since he didn't have a bike.

"Want something to drink?" I asked him.

"Good idea," he said. "I'll treat."

"You don't have to do that."

"Admission for the tour."

"Fine." I was still sore at him. It was as if he was looking for things to pick on. Searching with what Mom called a half-empty-glass attitude.

Inside the convenience store, Twig's mom worked the register. I hadn't been inside Allsup's since September, and it felt funny being around Mrs. Wagner. But she gave me the warmest smile when we entered the store, and when she rang us up, she said, "Girl, I miss you."

"I miss you, too." It came out in a whisper. That's all my throat could manage.

"Are you enjoying spring break?" she asked.

I nodded.

When we left, Joe asked, "Who is that lady?"

"Mrs. Wagner. I didn't introduce you because you didn't want to meet anyone."

"Wagner? Twig's mom?" Joe asked, but he might as well have said, *The hot girl's mom?*

I decided to tell him. He'd probably learn when he went to our school, and it might as well have come from me. "Twig and I used to be friends. I guess it wasn't a true friendship, as you would say."

"I don't know everything," he said, maybe because he could tell I was sad about the situation. Or maybe this was his way of apologizing. Or maybe he only wanted to know more about Twig.

"Mrs. Wagner is getting divorced. After September eleventh, she decided she didn't want to be married anymore."

Joe scowled. "What does that have to do with September eleventh?"

Even though my gut warned me not to say anything else, I explained anyway. "Well, that's what I heard. After September eleventh, she felt like life was too short to waste more time being married to someone she didn't want to be married to."

"That's stupid," he said.

"No," I said. "You don't understand. He really . . ." I stopped. Even if Twig and I weren't friends anymore, I didn't want to betray her.

Then Joe raised his voice. "I think it's stupid that people would use something really tragic as an excuse for their own selfish decisions."

I shouldn't have brought September 11 up. After

all, he was a New Yorker. The highway traffic buzzed behind us, and I was wishing I could be in one of those cars. The tour hadn't gone as I'd planned.

"I'm sorry," I said. "I know it must have been hard living so close to what happened."

"Yeah," he said. "And what is it with this town? They act like it happened here, with all the flags waving and painting that café red, white, and blue. They have no idea what it was really like! *You* have no idea! Almost everyone I know knew someone that died that day. Mr. Hampshire, who owns the store around the corner, his daughter died. Maggie, who works at the coffee shop, lost her husband. My teacher's brother, the postman's cousin. That day touched everyone. Everyone there. Not here."

I didn't know what to say, but I thought I should say something, and so I asked the most stupid question I could have asked. "Did you know anyone?"

Joe glared at me.

If I had only thought one moment before opening my big mouth.

He squinted and looked away. "Yeah, I did."

Just one moment. He faced me, and his eyes were wet. "I knew a few people. One of them was a great—" His voice broke.

Joe took a big breath and another, trying to steady his voice. Then he finished, "A really great guy. The bravest guy."

And then he walked away without saying another word.

Innis's
DRUG
STORE

Original Soda
Fountain Inside

CHAPTER 19

I wanted to tell him that I was sorry, but Joe had rushed away and was halfway down the street.

My head pounded, and my insides felt all jumbled up. The closer I got to the snow cone stand, the blurrier everything looked.

Dad stared in my direction while he waited on the customers who wore hiking boots and carried heavy backpacks. I went behind the stand and helped, filling the cups with grated ice while they talked to Dad about how they were walking to New Mexico from Dallas.

Usually Dad would have eaten that up, asked them all about it, but he nodded politely and stole glances at me.

"Stay safe out there," he told them after they settled up.

When the campers walked away, he asked, "What's wrong, Rylee?"

I stepped closer to him, and pressed my face against his T-shirt.

"It's okay," he said, patting my back. "Whatever it is, it's okay."

When I finished telling him what Joe had said and how I thought he was talking about his dad, he shook his head. "Poor kid. That explains a lot."

"What do you mean?"

"Why they moved to Antler, Texas, when they've never lived anywhere but New York. And Joe's anger."

"I don't think Joe likes me. I think he might even hate me now."

Dad lifted my chin. "Rylee, there's not a person in this town who doesn't like you."

I could think of one. Maybe two now.

"Joe's mad at the world," Dad said.

Two customers walked up and then three more. The line stayed short, but never slowed. I was thankful for that. We worked the busy hour together and then, when there was a lull, Dad got ready to head home.

"It's all yours," he said, "until your mom arrives."

"Are you going to tell Mom about Joe's dad?" I asked him. "Maybe he wasn't talking about his dad."

"They're our neighbors and new friends. I think she should know it's a possibility."

I gave a quick nod.

Dad changed the subject. "By the way, we're fully stocked with all the flavors now."

Right off, I noticed the two bottles of Burnt Marshmallow, which had proven a big hit. However Honey Pickle Juice had gotten gag reviews. It couldn't beat the classic, plain ol' Pickle Juice. I checked out the others, reading each label, searching for Blueberry.

A few moments after Dad left, I heard him signal to me with his familiar whistle. It sounded like a mockingbird call, five quick trills, followed by a long seesaw one. His whistle for Mayzee was a high-pitched, noisy killdeer's, but this one was mine.

I whistled back to him, because that was part of the ritual.

Dad stood at the edge of the square, giving me a thumbs-up sign.

I lifted my thumb.

≈

The next afternoon, on the way home from the stand, Mom and I saw Joe walking down the street toward us. Even from a distance, I recognized the Bowl-a-Rama Café T-shirt.

When our paths crossed, he said, "Hi." It came out in almost a whisper.

Mom greeted him with a sympathetic tone. "Hi, Joe."

Then she said, "I better head to the house." She turned to Joe. "Tell your mom hello for me."

I felt like a little girl wanting my mom to stay and rescue me from the awkward moment. Knowing Mom, that was probably why she took off. One of those you-can-handle-this moments. I swallowed and the lump slid down hard and rough.

"It looks like you got a job," I said.

"Yep." Joe yanked at his shirt. "I need to start earning some money. That way I can get a bike. I heard there's a cool pit where you can ride."

"Yeah, Gossimer Pit."

"The Ambassador of Antler didn't put that on her tour."

"I'm sorry," I blurted, but I wasn't apologizing about that. "I'm so sorry." Then softly, I asked, "Was it your dad?"

Joe stared down, nodded, and kicked low at the air like he was aiming for a pebble.

"That really sucks," I said.

He looked up then, kind of smiling. "That's the best thing anyone has ever said to me about what happened. You're right. It really does suck."

Something lifted inside me, and all at once I felt comfortable with Joe for the first time. We continued walking together, not speaking, not needing to, as the wind shook the leaves of the cottonwood trees that grew in the front yards along my street.

CHAPTER 20

Two thousand six hundred and six people died at the World Trade Center on September 11. Three hundred and forty-three were firefighters. Joe's dad was one of them.

The first day back to school from spring break, I kept an eye out for Joe. He never showed until last period, when I caught a glimpse of him with his mom in the office. She was probably registering him. Even from the back, I could tell he wasn't excited about being at school. A few feet away, he stood with his shoulders slouched and hands tucked in his pockets.

The next day I slowed my pace with Mayzee, hoping to see him before school, but I didn't catch sight of him until history class, when he beat me there. He sat in Twig's old seat, the one right next to mine. She'd long since moved to the back of class to sit between Vernon and Boone, while her former seat had remained empty like a reminder of our broken friendship.

Dad stood above him, showing him where we were in the textbook. When I sat, they both looked my way, smiling. Joe's was a nervous one. I gave him an encouraging smile back. It must have been hard to be the new kid. When my classmates entered and noticed Joe, they lowered their voices, whispering. Vernon came in with Twig. As usual, when he flopped in his chair, his big body caused the desk to move. Then he made such a loud display of adjusting it, moving it about, scraping the floor, that there was an almost perfect circle of scuffs on the linoleum.

Twig rerolled her army jacket cuffs, ignoring him. Attention-getting episodes never impressed her.

Why are you with him?

After calling roll, Dad got up from his desk and said, "Class, Joe Toscani is joining us. Please make him feel welcome."

That was it. No asking Joe to stand up or raise his hand. Everyone knew who the new kid was. If I were grading Dad's introduction, I'd give him an A-plus. No kid liked to have a big production made of such an awkward moment.

Dad got off his stool and wove between rows, circling the room as he spoke, causing us to twist around to see him. My neck always hurt when I left his class.

Every semester we were assigned a subject to write about, and since he'd taught seventh- and eighth-grade history for years, we knew what to expect. This semester we had to choose a person who was an important influence in the twentieth century. Dad asked one student a day to read their report until we'd heard the entire class. We never knew who he'd call on, so we had to be prepared.

That day, Dad asked, "Rylee, why don't you start us off?"

He could have warned me at breakfast. Didn't I get some privileges being the teacher's kid? I pushed the chair away from my desk, stood, and felt that stupid tickle. I cleared my throat.

I sounded like someone who'd swallowed a bug and couldn't cough it up. It was as if I were waving a flag, announcing NERVOUS PERSON HERE. But any of my classmates would have been a wreck reading in front of other kids if the teacher were their parent. Or in front of Joe. I felt like I was in a blackberry-pie-eating contest with my hands tied behind my back.

I read my opening. "Bill Monroe is considered the father of bluegrass. A mandolin player, singer, and songwriter, he created a style of music that continues to influence today's musicians such as Marty Stuart, Ricky Skaggs, and Chris Thile."

My report had taken me weeks to research and write, and I believed it was good. I knew it was good. Most of my classmates coasted. Some practically plagiarized their reports from the library's ancient encyclopedias.

There I was, standing in front of what seemed like the whole world. After the first sentence, I had to clear my throat again, but halfway through my report, I relaxed a little, became braver and more confident. The rest of the reading went smoother.

When I'd finished, I looked up at Dad and could tell he thought my report was good, too, because of the way he tried not to smile. His eyes looked like I'd won an Olympic medal.

Dad cleared his throat. Apparently I'd inherited the family tic.

From the back of the room, Twig gave me a blank stare.

"Thank you, Rylee." Then Dad turned to my classmates. "Any questions for her?"

Vernon's hand shot up.

Dad called on him. "Yes, Mr. Clifton?"

"I wanted to ask Rylee if her dad helped with her homework?"

"No." I sat down, humiliated.

After school Joe came over to me while I waited for slowpoke Mayzee. "Vernon is a jerk."

"First day at school, and you already have him pegged."

"I had him figured out the first night we worked together. What does Twig see in him?"

I pretended I didn't hear his question.

~

I couldn't wait for school each morning. Joe was in half of my classes, and he sat with the Garcia twins and me at lunch.

Frederica had a crush on him. I knew right off when, after Joe's first day, she came to school with her hair down and legs shaved, with a couple of bandages above each ankle.

Joe's eyes glazed over whenever Juan Leon talked about math, but he politely slipped in "hmm" and "really" every once in a while.

By Joe's third day, though, he interrupted Juan Leon. "Man, I'm glad you like math, but I really don't think I'll be using it much after I graduate."

Juan Leon frowned. "Of course you will."

"No," Joe said, "I really don't think so. Well, maybe to count my money."

"How about deductive reasoning?" Juan Leon asked.

Joe's forehead wrinkled. "Say what?"

Great thought. Now he's invited Juan Leon to get on a math tangent that will leave us even more exhausted and confused.

Juan Leon put down his sandwich and straightened his back. "Deductive reasoning is the process a person uses to make conclusions based on previously known facts."

Joe shook his head.

"You'll use it," Juan Leon said. "Believe me."

THE MYRTIE MAE PRUITT
PUBLIC LIBRARY
April 6th 2002

CHAPTER 21

The groundbreaking for the new library was on Saturday, so Mom and Dad decided not to open the stand until after the ceremony. Dad was giving a speech on behalf of the building committee. Our family showed up dressed in our Sunday best. The whole town seemed to have turned out, including Joe and his mom. Some people stood while others sat in lawn chairs like they were waiting for a Fourth of July parade. There hadn't been a new building in Antler since before I was born.

Maybe before Mom and Dad were born. This was a big deal.

Across the street, Twig perched on a curb. I wanted to check out her reaction when Joe came over and stood by me. Unfortunately Vernon joined her at the same time.

Joe had noticed Twig and Vernon. They sat so closely their legs were touching. I hoped Joe noticed that, too.

Twig lifted her hand, and for a quick second, it looked like she was going to wave at us.

I raised my hand to wave back.

But she wasn't waving. She was merely tucking a lock of hair behind her ear.

Embarrassed, I quickly did the same.

The crowd quieted because Dad was standing at the podium and had begun his speech. "This library was the dream of one woman, who wanted our citizens to have a better library so that we, too, could dream. Miss Myrtie Mae Pruitt loved this town. We see that love in her photography. We see it in her generous gift."

Dad unveiled a plaque with today's date and the

library's name—THE MYRTIE MAE PRUITT PUBLIC LIBRARY. Everyone applauded.

The mayor was having trouble shoveling a scoop of the dry dirt. So Dad assisted him, breaking the ground with the sharp end and handing the shovel back to the mayor, who was still only able to scrape up a tablespoon of dirt.

It was funny how I'd passed this lot forever and never noticed it. Now, by the end of the year, it would be a place where I'd probably spend a lot of time.

Our current library was run by volunteers and had short hours with weird closings like CLOSED FOR FAIR DAYS AND PRESIDENTIAL ELECTIONS. I wouldn't have been surprised if I'd seen a CLOSED, GONE FISHING sign. Thanks to Miss Myrtie Mae, there'd be a real librarian working here. Dad said they'd already received a few résumés, some from as far away as Iowa. It was nice to know some people wanted to live in Antler. I wished Joe were one of them.

After the ceremony, we opened the stand, offering the large size at half price because of the special occasion. The whole town seemed to be in a cheerful mood as they lined up, causing our biggest rush ever. We quickly ran out of Bahama Mama syrup because a lot of people ordered them for nostalgic reasons. For a good hour, the grinding of the ice machine and swooshing of cups being filled couldn't drown out the chatter and laughter. Syrup splashes spotted my Sunday dress, but I didn't care.

Buster had been the first person in line, and after he was finished eating, he returned to the line and waited for another turn.

"Back for seconds, Buster?" I asked.

He shook his head. "No. Um, can I have a job?"

The line was still long, and I quickly said, "I'm sorry, Buster, this isn't a good time. Can you come back another day?"

"Sure, boss. I'll come back after my birthday." He walked away, then he turned around and yelled, "Go, Mustangs!"

When the crowd finally died and we sat on crates to catch our breaths, Dad told us, "I think this is what I'd call a Wylie Womack Day."

"Do you want a snow cone, Mr. Wilson," Mom teased, "for old times' sake?"

Dad's tie was already loose, but he pulled it off then and slung it over his shoulder. "No, Mrs. Wilson, I don't believe I do."

At home, I opened my top bedside drawer and pulled out the manila envelope with Miss Myrtie Mae's pictures. I hadn't touched them since that quick look-over the day Opa and I picked them up from the drugstore. I spread them out along the bed, and when it was completely covered, I started placing them around the floor, leaving a path of carpet.

Many were close-ups of household items—a comb, hairbrush, bottles of prescribed pills, stacks of books, a painting on a wall. Others revealed scenes from outside the first-story window of her bedroom. There were some photos of the massive magnolia tree in her front yard during different seasons—the winter snow covering the emerald leaves, the spring shedding of the yellow ones, the abundant white blooms of summer, and the brown cones with red seeds in the fall.

A few of the photos showed people walking by. Why hadn't I examined them closer before? Now I studied the faces—there was Dad, pushing the lawnmower around her yard, Mr. Pham approaching her home with a bouquet, Mom and her friends power walking on the street out front, the mailman with his satchel of mail slung over his shoulder.

I slowed down, looking at each photo carefully, laughing at discovering one of Twig and me as second graders, riding our bikes. I lifted the picture, bringing it near my face. Our long hair was blowing in the wind, and we had wide grins on our faces. I held that picture a long time, gazing at it, wanting to go back to that very moment. That moment when *squim*, *tob*, and *drin* meant something.

There were almost three hundred pictures there. I studied the self-portrait of Miss Myrtie Mae again, now realizing it was of her reflection in the dresser mirror. She was sitting in her bed, wearing a quilted bed jacket, holding her camera above her waist. Uncombed hair, so thin some of her scalp was showing. Droopy bags under her sunken eyes. Prominent cheekbones. She wasn't smiling, but she didn't appear sad either. The photo felt so true, so real, it was beautiful. She was beautiful.

These were the last photos Miss Myrtie Mae took. Even when she was sick and frail, she never stopped taking pictures. It was something she truly loved. I wondered what it would be like to love doing something that much. As if someone heard my question, the sound of a mandolin danced through my thoughts. And it wasn't Chris Thile playing or Ricky Skaggs or Marty Stuart or any of the other mandolin players I admired. It was me.

I had loved playing the mandolin. From the first moment I heard a bluegrass song, I'd been under the spell of its soulful sound. And when Opa gave me my great-grandfather's mandolin and taught me to play "You Are My Sunshine," I'd felt a part of something. I hadn't been great at it, but I hadn't been awful either.

I'd practiced the song over and over until I thought I was good enough to show Twig. When I did, it was a night she'd slept over. The whole time we ate dinner, I kept playing the song in my head so much my fingertips moved, pressing and strumming imaginary strings underneath the table.

Later when we were washing dishes, Dad kissed

the back of Mom's neck. It wasn't the first time. Although that night I was embarrassed by the way they were carrying on. Twig stared at their backs, frowning.

"Let's go to my room," I'd said. "I want to show you something."

I took out the mandolin and looked over to my Nickel Creek poster. It was as if the trio were cheering, "You can do it, Rylee Wilson!"

When I began to play, Twig fell back on the bed and cracked up.

She pinched her nose and sang, "Twang, twang, twang!"

My whole body felt like it had cracked in half. I stopped and put the mandolin away. "Want to go outside?" I asked.

Once there, she cartwheeled across the entire backyard. After she finished, she said, "Your turn."

I'd tried a million times, but had never been able to do a cartwheel. She'd known that.

Now, looking at Miss Myrtie Mae's pictures covering my bed and floor, I realized I'd stopped doing something

I loved because Twig hadn't approved. I quickly gathered the photos and returned them to their envelope, opened the closet door, and pulled out my mandolin case.

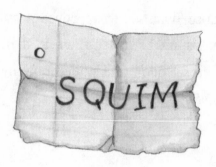

CHAPTER 22

I guess Opa had never given up hope that I'd return to it, because she'd never asked for her dad's mandolin back. The day after I decided to pick up the mandolin again, I walked into the opry, carrying my case.

Opa was standing at the concession counter, writing the program for the next show. She looked up, smiled, and let go of her pencil. "Do you want to start with the bar chords or do you want to warm up with something sweet and simple?"

My great-grandfather, Tater Benson, had been in a traveling band called the Prairie Pickers, and he'd taught Opa to play practically every string instrument. One of her opry night songs always showcased that talent, when she'd move from band member to band member and they'd hand over their instruments to her. By the end of the song, she'd played the guitar, banjo, mandolin, and fiddle. The audience members went wild for it, sometimes even getting on their feet and clapping along.

Returning to the mandolin changed the way I listened to music. I slept with my iPod and earbuds under my pillow. As usual, I awoke before anyone else, but now Nickel Creek kept me company. I loved every song on the album, but I hit replay whenever "Sweet Afton" came on, listening to the old Scottish tune a dozen times before I went to sleep.

After school, I practiced the mandolin in my closet, softly strumming and barely picking the strings. Except for Opa, I wasn't ready to let my family know I was playing again. They'd been disappointed when I put it down—even Mayzee was. When they heard me again, I wanted to be great, maybe perfect.

All week after school, Joe waited with me for Mayzee. I liked how people saw us together. Especially when Twig and Vernon passed us on Wednesday and I caught Twig's sneaky sideways glance.

Joe saw too. "Man, you two really know how to hold a grudge."

"Why do you say that?" I asked.

"You don't even look at each other straight on."

"Have you heard from your Brooklyn friend?" I hated myself for hoping he would say no.

"His name is Arham. Yeah, we've talked almost every day. We'll email once our computer gets connected to the Internet."

My cheeks felt prickly like a pincushion. "Must be nice."

"When it's connected, you can use it anytime you want." He thought I was talking about the computer.

"Hey," he said, "I've been thinking about Zachary."

"Zachary Beaver?"

"Yeah. Why don't you find out where he is? Surprise your dad. That way they might reunite."

"Oh, I don't know about that. Dad thinks it's best not to find out."

"I don't get that. You said they were friends. Seems like he'd want to know the guy's okay, especially after all these years."

I repeated what Dad told me, about how making friends with Zachary was the best part of a bad summer and how he wanted to remember him like that.

"How bad?" Joe asked. "Because I had a really bad summer."

"I don't know what he meant. He didn't tell me and I guess I thought it was better not to ask. Zachary might not be around anymore." I avoided the word *dead* with Joe like Dad avoided the word *fat* when he talked about Zachary.

"Well, I don't see how it could hurt for you to find out about him," Joe said. "If it's bad news, you don't have to tell him."

"I'll think about it." I wondered if Twig ever thought about when things were good between us.

～

Friday, as we waited for Mayzee, Joe told me, "Your Uncle Cal has a crush on my mom."

"What?"

"He asked her out. Can you believe it?" Joe didn't sound happy.

"What did she say?"

He looked at me like I'd asked a stupid question. "She turned him down, of course."

"He might not know about your dad." Maybe Dad should have told him.

"Well, he needs to back off. He left flowers for her on the doorstep this morning."

"That doesn't sound like him." Uncle Cal was cheap. Mom and Dad teased him about it all the time.

"Well, he didn't leave a card, but I know they must have been from him."

Mayzee appeared out of the school and took her sweet time, talking to a friend. I hollered her name.

Joe slung his backpack over a shoulder. "Have you thought any more about Zachary?"

I wondered why Joe was so obsessed with finding him. I yelled for Mayzee to hurry. "Maybe he doesn't want to be found," I said.

Mayzee finally started toward us.

"Maybe he does," Joe said. "Maybe Zachary wants to know his friendship mattered."

CHAPTER 23

Uncle Cal made an announcement that evening at our Lasagna Night.

"Well, you should all be happy for me. I think I have a new girl."

"Who's the lucky lady?" Mom sounded bored. It wasn't like we hadn't been through this before. His last wife left him broke and depressed. He was at our house every night for months. Then when he did start dating again, he fell hard for every one of the ladies.

"Our new neighbor is sweet on me," Uncle Cal said, "but a little shy about it."

"Joe's mom?" My voice squeaked the words.

"Yep, I do believe she left me some flowers, trying to make up for turning me down earlier when I asked her out for a steak dinner."

"Are you sure?" I was ready to set him straight, but now I was confused.

Uncle Cal peeked at the lasagna in the oven. "I asked her to dinner. She politely said, no, thank you. When I got home from work, I found a bouquet of flowers waiting for me on the doorstep."

"Did you give her flowers?" I asked, trying to solve the mystery.

"Heck, no!" Uncle Cal said, insulted.

Everyone cracked up except Mayzee, who wanted to know what was so funny.

Mom explained. "Mayzee, Uncle Cal has never given any woman flowers. He's too cheap."

"Why should I," Uncle Cal asked, "if they give them to me?"

Dad shook his head. "Cal, Maria probably didn't

give you those flowers. Besides, her husband just died. Tragically. Remember what I told you?"

"I remember," Uncle Cal said, "but maybe she's ready to move on. Maybe she wants to be happy again."

Mom chimed in. "You might want to hold back a little this time."

"Call me optimistic," Uncle Cal said, "and apparently irresistible."

I couldn't wait to tell Joe that there was an anonymous admirer leaving flowers on doorsteps. Maybe Antler had their very own Cupid.

Joe laughed when I told him Uncle Cal wasn't the person who left his mom the flowers and he'd received a bouquet too. He was hanging out with me while I worked my shift.

"It's weird! There must be some secret admirer in town," I said. "Or maybe two."

He cracked up again.

"What's so funny? Am I missing something?"

Joe recovered. "*I* left the flowers on Cal's steps."

"I don't understand. Why would you do that?"

"They were the ones on our porch that I thought

Cal had left for my mom. So I returned them to send a message."

"Oh, he got a message all right. He thinks your mom left them for him because she turned him down for dinner."

Joe snapped his fingers. "Man, I messed that whole thing up. How can I fix this?"

I shrugged.

"Maybe you could tell him my mom didn't leave them," Joe said.

"I'm staying out of it." Uncle Cal had been so excited thinking Mrs. Toscani had given them. Maybe there was a small chance for a romance there.

Joe nodded. "Yeah, you're right. It will work itself out. But I wonder who's sending flowers to her?"

"Your mom is pretty," I said. "She must have a lot of admirers."

"She's a mom. Looks like a mom. Acts like a mom."

"She's not everyone's mom," I told him.

We Remember
9-11-01

CHAPTER 24

Joe had worked at the Bowl-a-Rama Café as a pin-setter for two weeks now. Every weekend after work, he dropped by for a snow cone. Last Saturday his lips were Grateful Dead Grape. Today they were Dreamsicle Orange. He hadn't ordered Blueberry once.

He was sitting atop the picnic table, his legs dangling off the side while he told me how Ferris's jukebox played ancient twangy music. He said he'd almost learned the hard way to quickly raise his legs behind the pins when a fast ball started rolling down the lane. I listened to him explain all about ninepin bowling, how it started in Germany and how there were only a few places in Texas where it was available. I knew all of this, of course. He'd probably forgotten what Ferris said about my being in a bowling club. But it was good to hear Joe talk with enthusiasm about something in Antler.

After a carload of college students from West Texas A&M left the stand, Joe dug in his jeans pocket and pulled out an index card. "I found this used bike for sale posted on Ferris's bulletin board. Do you know where this is?"

Right off I saw the name Levi Fetterman by the address. "Yeah, that's Sheriff Levi."

"He's the sheriff?"

"He was. Now he runs a dog shelter a mile out of town across the railroad tracks. If you want, I'll take you there after I'm off work."

～

On the way to Sheriff Levi's, Joe told me he'd finally gotten as fast as Vernon setting pins. Ferris told Joe privately that he was good for business because he'd never seen Vernon move so quick until he hired Joe.

A dirt road ran along the other side of the railroad tracks. We hadn't been walking on it long when we passed a little blue house with a marker that read CHILD-HOOD HOME OF JUAN GARCIA, CHAMPION PGA GOLFER.

"Really? He grew up here?"

"Yeah, he's Juan Leon and Frederica's uncle. Have you seen him play on the sports channel?"

"I don't watch golf. I know who Tiger Woods is, though. Where does Juan Garcia live now?"

"Florida."

Joe nodded knowingly. "Guess he couldn't wait to get out of this town."

I'd hoped things were changing for Joe, that maybe he'd started to see himself being happy here, but it was probably too soon.

The wildflowers had started to emerge, poking their heads above the tall grass in the fields near the tracks. The Engelmann daisies with their yellow petals waved at us as we passed. By summer they would have grown to almost knee-high.

"Look at all the weeds," Joe said. "In Brooklyn, you get fined if you don't keep your grass mowed."

"I think they're pretty," I said. "I love wildflowers."

Halfway to Sheriff Levi's, we heard dogs barking in the distance.

"How many dogs does he have?"

"It depends. Most of them are dogs that people have dumped along the highway. Fair warning—he'll try to get you to take one home."

Sheriff Levi's house was an old gray ranch with a line of cedars planted at the edge of his property for a windbreak. An oversize peach tree grew too close to the front door with branches crisscrossing over the roof. As we neared his place, we saw dogs lying around the property in a fenced-in area. All shapes and sizes, from a teacup poodle to a German shepherd mix, came up to the front of the fence and barked, barked, barked.

A small terrier type with an underbite had somehow escaped. He came over to Joe and sniffed his sneakers.

Joe reached down and scratched his head. "Hey, fella. You sure are ugly."

"That's not nice," I said, but he was right. The dog was so ugly he was cute.

The little dog rolled over. Joe squatted and rubbed his belly.

The others dogs continued barking.

I squatted too. "Hey, puppy."

The dog paid me no mind.

"I guess I'm not that interesting," I said.

"You have to be a belly rubber," Joe told me.

The dog's ears flopped, and his tongue hung out of the corner of his mouth. He actually looked like he was grinning.

Every dog started to howl when Sheriff Levi appeared on the porch, wearing a dirty cowboy hat, a stiffly starched shirt, and faded jeans. His stature was long, bony, and a little stooped. He went to the edge of the porch, cupped his hands around his mouth, and sang out in a high-pitched yodel, adding his part to the dog chorus. "Yi—ppy-yi-yo!"

The dogs continued while Sheriff Levi threw back his head and howled with them.

Then as if remembering he wasn't a dog, Sheriff Levi stood military style with his arms at his side and ordered, "At ease!"

The dogs quieted.

Clearly impressed, Joe kept looking over at me, but

I'd been here before. This was Sheriff Levi's way of saying "howdy."

Then the dog whisperer called out to me, "Rylee Wilson, is that you?"

"Yes, sir."

Sheriff Levi was in front of us now, teetering a little on his skinny legs. He'd gotten so old, and his right eye still twitched. "Haven't seen you in a while. I need to go in town and get a Bahama Mama soon. Who's your friend?"

"This is Joe."

"Hi," Joe said.

Sheriff Levi held out his hand, and Joe surprised me. He took hold and gave Sheriff Levi's hand a shake—not a firm one, but at least he made an effort.

"Joe, hope you liked our welcome."

Joe smiled and nodded.

"Did you come here for a dog?" Sheriff Levi asked.

"No," Joe said. "A bike." He glanced around, but the only bike leaning against the house was old and a little rusty on the fenders.

"That's it," Sheriff Levi said. "I put a new chain on it. It could use a new paint job, though."

And more. I wanted to tell Joe to skip this one. Maybe Dad would sell him his, since he hadn't ridden it in years.

Joe walked over to it. "Is it still thirty dollars?"

"If you take a dog, I'll give it to you for free."

"I'm sorry. I really don't want a dog."

"Then it's twenty dollars," Sheriff Levi said.

Joe squinted. "I thought the ad said thirty dollars."

"Ten dollars off on account of your good taste in friends." Sheriff Levi winked at me, or maybe it was just the twitch.

"Thanks." Joe uncurled his thin roll of cash and peeled away some bills.

"Don't you want to try it out first?" I asked him.

"You're welcome to," Sheriff Levi said. "Might be a good idea."

"Nah, I trust you."

"So be it. Sold."

Before we took off, Sheriff Levi insisted that we see the photograph Miss Myrtie Mae left him. We waited while he went into the house and brought out the picture of a hound dog sitting in the back seat of the sheriff's car peering through the criminal bars. "That was

Duke, one of my favorite dogs. Found him walking around the square."

I told him about the Zachary Beaver picture Miss Myrtie Mae left Dad.

"Goodness gracious, I think of that boy every now and then. I've always been partial to orphans. I wonder if he's still alive."

"I wish I knew," I said.

"If he is," Sheriff Levi said, "he might live in Florida."

"Hey, maybe Juan Garcia knows?" Joe joked.

Sheriff Levi thought Joe was being serious. "Oh, I doubt that. Garcia is too busy on the PGA tour. The reason I suggested Florida is there's a little town there where a lot of circus and sideshow people live when they aren't traveling. Come to think of it, I haven't heard of any sideshows in years. He may be retired."

Sheriff Levi opened the front door, placed the picture against the wall, and stepped back out. "Zachary might live in New York City. I believe that was where he was from. Somewhere around those parts."

"Really?" Joe would never stop bugging me about finding Zachary Beaver now.

"Joe's from New York City," I told Sheriff Levi.

He faced Joe. "Are you the boy who's living with his mom in Miss Myrtie Mae's house?"

"Well, I guess it's ours now," Joe said.

Sheriff Levi nodded. "Yep, yep, that's right."

"We lived in Brooklyn," Joe told him.

"Sorry you had to go through all that craziness that went on there. What's the world coming to?"

Joe turned and walked away fast with the bike at his side like he was trying to forget Sheriff Levi's comment. "Thanks for the bike," he said, but he didn't turn around.

"Thanks, Sheriff Levi. Come by the stand when you can." I rushed off to catch up with Joe.

The little dog raced past me and reached Joe before I did. Joe stopped walking, and stared down. "Sorry, little guy. You can't come home with me."

Sheriff Levi reached us and scooped the dog into his arms. "Sure you don't want a dog, Joe?"

Joe shook his head and began moving forward, guiding the bike again.

Petting the runaway's head, Sheriff Levi turned to

me, and said, "Tell your parents hello and that I'll be getting that snow cone before the week's out."

I jogged up to Joe's side, afraid that Sheriff Levi's comment would set us back to the rough part of our new friendship. I wasn't good at filling these pauses, but I took a stab. "You don't think your mom would let you have a dog?"

"Sure, she'd probably let me," he answered, "but I don't want a dog."

"I'd have one, but Mom and Mayzee are allergic to them."

"Dogs die," he said.

The wind picked up, blowing a tumbleweed across our path. Down the road ahead dozens of them rolled until they reached the raised track.

"Wow!" Joe said. "Where do they come from?"

Tumbleweeds were nothing new to me. They looked mighty rolling across the prairie and the highways, but as soon as they hit something big, they fell apart.

One night, right before a snowstorm, Mom and I were driving back from Oklahoma. Giant tumbleweeds, as big as bales of hay, seemed to come out of nowhere as they rolled in front of our car. We'd squealed each time one crossed our way, but we drove right through them, scattering them into a million tiny sticks.

Joe tilted his chin and peered at me sideways. "So, Ambassador, are you going to teach me to ride this bike?"

CHAPTER 25

"You don't know how to ride a bike?"

"Nope." Joe wasn't embarrassed. "My mom saw a guy flip over and hit his head when she was pregnant with me. She thinks it was a sign that I shouldn't ever learn."

"My mom and dad have always made me wear a helmet," I told him. "It was green and the other kids used to call me Martian. Then Sheriff Levi started giving out coupons for an ice cream cone from the Dairy Queen to any kid he caught wearing a helmet. After that, it was cool."

"Well, I guess I better wear a helmet, then. I like ice cream cones. Ready for my first lesson?"

The dirt road that ran along the railroad track was a perfect place for teaching someone how to ride a bike. The only people who could possibly see us were the cars speeding up as they left Antler.

Joe straddled the bike, and I steadied it by gripping the seat.

"Okay," I said.

"Okay?" he asked.

"I mean *go!*"

I still had hold of the bike seat while he put his feet on the pedals. When he pressed down, I let go. Joe started out wobbly—going slow, too slow.

He fell.

"That's okay. Nice first try." I tried to sound encouraging.

He bounced up, brushed himself off, and got back on.

Come on, I thought, *faster, faster.* Joe didn't remind

me of someone who would be cautious at anything. But that was the way he pedaled. Then he fell.

I rushed over to him. "Are you okay?"

He nodded and jumped back on, returning to his slow pedaling. He fell again, and again. And again. Guaranteed bruises.

"If you pick up the speed early on, you won't wobble and fall," I told him.

I'd never taught anyone to ride a bike. Mayzee still used training wheels. This was hard.

On the next attempt, Joe increased his speed from the start, and he was off.

"Yes!" I yelled.

Smooth sailing. It was as if those falls had never happened.

Ka-nuck, ka-nuck, ka-nuck. The train was up the track from us but soon parallel. Joe waved his arm high, and the engineer sounded the long, vibrating whistle. *Wooo-wooo. Ka-nuck, ka-nuck, ka-nuck.*

Then Joe stretched both arms toward the sky and pedaled hands free. Now he was racing the train. I sprinted, trying to catch up, but Joe kept pedaling faster. He gripped the handlebars, leaned back, and did a wheelie. If it weren't for the earlier falls, I'd have sworn he was bluffing me.

Breathless, I focused on the tip of his braid, which was blowing in the wind like a clock pendulum.

Joe was a quick learner. A few minutes before, he had no balance. Now he was coasting down the path with me trailing way behind and the last train cars whizzing by.

"How do you stop?" he yelled, without turning around.

I quit running so I could speak. "Squeeze the brakes under your handles!"

He looked down, moving.

"They don't work!" he hollered.

Joe slowed to a tricycle pace, let go of the bike, raised his arms and dove sideways, landing mere feet away from the track. He sprawled out flat, kissing the ground as the train sped by.

I rushed up to him. "I'm sorry. I should have told you how to stop before you started."

He rolled over onto his back. No bruises, but his

cheeks and nose were smudged with dirt. "It doesn't matter. The brakes are shot."

"Good thing your mom's not here."

Joe started to laugh and held up his arms. "Help me up."

I gave him a good yank until he was sitting on the ground, where I joined him. I pointed to my cheeks.

He raised his eyebrows like he didn't understand.

"Um . . . you have a little dirt," I explained.

"Oh," he said. Then he wiped his face with the back of his sleeve. "Gone?"

I nodded.

"Should I get my money back from that shyster?" he asked.

"Sheriff Levi's not a shyster. He probably didn't know. I doubt he's ever ridden a bike. But how did you—"

"I'm kidding. He's a little loony, though, in a good way. Surely somebody can fix bicycle brakes around here."

"I know someone who can fix bikes, but I don't think you like him."

"Vernon?"

Then I laughed. "No, Uncle Cal. He's a cyclist and

pretty good at stuff like that. He thinks it's fun. Dad told me when Uncle Cal was a kid, he took apart his bicycle so he could put it back together again."

"I didn't say I didn't like him. I just don't want him hitting on my mom."

"Okay, then," I told him. "Let's stop by his place on the way back. He's probably home by now. Are you going to say anything to him about the flowers?"

"Nah." He smiled. "He might mess up my brakes."

At the next turnoff, we crossed the railroad tracks and then the highway. We passed the Dairy Queen and reached the square. This felt like old times with Twig. Every day had seemed like an adventure.

"How did you know how to do all those brave stunts—riding without your hands and then that wheelie?"

Joe shrugged. "Beginner's luck."

I wondered if there was more to it than that.

~

After Joe's first riding lesson, we walked over to Uncle Cal's home and met him as he pulled in the driveway. He told Joe he'd fix his brakes after work the next week.

"Rylee says you cycle?" Joe said it like he wasn't that interested.

"Every day," Uncle Cal said. "If you ever want to join me, I ride around the town in the morning, right before dawn."

"I'm not a morning person," Joe told him, throwing in a fake yawn.

Uncle Cal got on Joe's bike and tried out the brakes. "I'll give you a holler when I'm finished."

I started to leave, but Joe nudged me with his elbow. "Why don't you ask him about Zachary?"

I halfway shrugged.

Uncle Cal straightened his posture. "What's that?"

"Dad doesn't really want to find out what happened to him. He says he wants to remember him like he was. That it had been a bad summer and Zachary Beaver was the best part."

Uncle Cal grimaced. Then he took off his cap and wiped the sweat from his brow before replacing it. "Yeah, that was the summer of seventy-one, the summer my brother, Wayne, died over in Vietnam."

"I'm sorry," I barely whispered the words. "I knew about Wayne, but I didn't know when he—"

Joe looked away, shading his eyes as if he were on the lookout for something.

"It was a long time ago, Rylee," Uncle Cal said. "Still miss him, though. Even now, whenever I ride out to the canyon overlook and there's not a soul out there, I scream, 'Wayne McKnight, I miss you!' It feels like my words fly straight up to heaven."

Joe faced us again, and I could tell he was taking it all in.

"I wish I'd known him," I said.

"No one like him." Uncle Cal turned away from us, but not before I heard the choke in his voice.

CHAPTER 26

The following Sunday, Joe called to tell me Uncle Cal had finished fixing the brakes. "Want to meet me over there?"

My shift wouldn't start for another hour, so I got on my bike and headed across the street. Joe was already making the corner.

"You run fast!" I told him, hopping off my bike.

"I used to run track," he said, speeding to a halt. He wore old bowling shoes—burgundy and green with the number eight.

"Antler has a track team. Maybe you can be on it."

He frowned. "I don't know how I would do it without Arham. We always paced each other. By the way, you do kind of look like a Martian."

"Huh?"

He tapped my helmet.

"It's pink," I said. "Martians are green."

"Who knows if Martians are green?"

"My dad said you could use his helmet until you get one."

When Joe didn't respond, I said, "It would probably make your mom feel better after what happened."

Joe frowned. "What do you mean?"

"The accident she saw before you were born?"

"Oh. Yeah."

"What did your mom say about the bike?"

"Well, I'm working on it."

We walked together down the McKnights' long driveway. It ended a few yards before Uncle Cal's mobile home, where he stood next to a shiny bike. Not only had Uncle Cal fixed the brakes, he'd given it a new paint job, too.

We stared at the metallic blue finish.

"Is that the same bike?" Joe asked.

"Oh, I gave it a spit shine." Uncle Cal took out a cloth from his back pocket and wiped an imaginary smudge on the back fender.

"Man! Thanks," Joe said. "You didn't have to do that."

"I know. But I did."

"What do I owe you?"

"Owe me?" Uncle Cal scowled. "Well, could you get me a pair of those spiffy shoes?"

"Ferris said I could have them," said Joe. "He was going to throw them out, but I think they're cool. Comfortable, too."

"I'm kidding. That's not my style." Uncle Cal was one of those Texans who wore cowboy boots almost every day.

"Well, thanks, again," Joe said.

He seemed uncomfortable saying it. Maybe it was hard to say thank you for something his dad might have done had he been alive. Or maybe because Joe couldn't forget that Uncle Cal was crushing on his mom.

"You should let me pay you," Joe said, walking the bike down the driveway.

"Just wear a helmet," Uncle Cal said before he went back inside.

When Uncle Cal disappeared, Joe asked, "How about that Gossimer Pit? Or is that a rumor?"

"Follow me," I told him. "But I can't stay long. I have to report to work soon."

We pedaled to the western edge of town, where Allsup's sat, and turned south. The dried-up small playa lake was located in a field. One of the old NO FISH-ING, NO SWIMMING signs was still posted. It was ten feet at the deepest, and sometimes it did almost fill up if we had some heavy rains. But that was rare. When Mr. Gossimer was alive, he kept it filled with a hose connected to his well. But there hadn't been any complaints since it had become a pit.

Joe stared at the bicycle tread patterns creating a mosaic covering the surface. I had a hunch I knew what he was thinking, that this wasn't what he thought the pit would be, that there was something better in New York.

"Well?" I said.

A big grin spread across his face. "Awesome!"

Finally something from Antler had impressed him. It felt like a door opening. Maybe it would lead to something else that might make him happy here.

"Ready?" I asked.

We rode and rode, crisscrossing the pit. At some point, Joe got carried away and did a wheelie. Then he checked my reaction and fell.

I jumped off my bike and rushed over to him.

He brushed himself off, then he sprang to his feet. "Well," he said, "are you ready to start on our project?"

"What project?"

"The Zachary Beaver Project."

I let out a big sigh and glanced down at my watch. My work shift would start in five minutes.

"What are you afraid of?" Joe asked. "That he'll tell you he hated Antler? Couldn't wait to get away?"

"No," I said firmly. "My dad could be right. Something could have happened to him."

"Well, if it did, you don't have to tell him. It would probably only take a phone call. And think about how happy your dad would be if you found him and everything was great. Maybe Zachary lost weight. Maybe he's a runner."

"Or maybe he's not."

"Maybe he was in the Olympics," Joe said.

"Or maybe he wasn't."

"But he could have had a fabulous life. He might regret that they haven't stayed in touch."

"I wouldn't even know where to begin. He traveled around the country. He was a sideshow act. Long-distance phone calls cost a fortune. Do you really think finding him is only one phone call away?"

"Maybe he's in Florida like Sheriff Levi mentioned."

I didn't say anything.

"What's the worst that could happen? You find out he's dead, and you don't tell your dad. But if he's alive and doing well, then you might make him happy to have found an old friend. I'd feel that way about Arham."

"How long have you been friends?"

"Forever."

I wanted to say, *Don't expect him to remain the same person. He could change.*

"Our dads worked together," Joe said. "It's been hard for him since it all happened, especially since they're Muslim."

"His dad's a fireman?"

"No," he said, a little miffed. "He *was*. By the way, in New York they let Muslims be firemen."

My right foot rested on a pedal, then I quickly removed it. Then I put it back. Talking to Joe sometimes felt like walking in a minefield. One wrong move could set off an explosion. And I felt guilty whenever he talked about what had happened, what he'd lost. I felt guilty because my dad was here.

"So how about the project?" Joe straddled his bike, waiting for an answer.

I was so relieved that he'd changed the subject that I said, "Okay, let's find Zachary."

ESTATE
SALE
Saturday, September 15
8:00 am - 6:00 pm
All proceeds will go to
the new Antler Public Library
BURGESS AUCTION HOUSE

CHAPTER 27

If someone wanted a copy of *Pride and Prejudice* or a
Zane Grey western or an unreliable computer, they could
find it at the Antler Public Library. And that's what we
found Thursday, the day we started our search for Zachary
Beaver. Most of the library volunteers only worked one
day a month, and today was Miss Earline's day.

"Service is down," she said when we asked if we
could use the computer.

"That figures," I said to Joe as we left the library.

"I wish my mom would hurry and get Internet service," Joe said. "She hasn't even called anyone about it yet. Don't you have any friends who have a computer?"

"Juan Leon and Frederica are the only ones who I know, but if the library doesn't have service today, they won't either. Welcome to small town technology."

We needed to go to the big city. Opa said she'd drop Joe and me off at the Amarillo Public Library after our Saturday breakfast.

~

That morning I stared out my south window toward Joe's window. It was before dawn, and a lamp cast an orange glow on his closed curtains. I watched his room for a moment, trying to catch a glimpse of a shadow, but there was no movement. Then a figure on a bicycle rode up to the corner and stopped. Joe straddled his bike, looking out ahead as if he was waiting for something or someone.

I rushed over to my north window and looked out toward Uncle Cal's place, but there was no sign of him. Back and forth I went, checking from window to window, watching Joe wait for Uncle Cal. A minute or two passed. Then Joe gave up and pedaled home. A few seconds later, I heard the quick short clicks of a bicycle. Then I watched Uncle Cal ride down his driveway and turn east as he did every morning.

～

At eight, Opa picked me up in Delta Dawn, and we drove over to Joe's house. When Mrs. Toscani answered the door, she must have noticed me staring at the stacks of unopened moving boxes. "I had to take a little break from unpacking."

It looked as if she'd hardly begun. According to Mom, she hadn't started her job search yet either.

Once outside, Joe noticed Delta Dawn right off. "Cool car!"

Should have known a boy who wore scuffed bowling shoes wouldn't mind riding in a car the color of Pepto Bismol. I didn't mention seeing him on his bike earlier that morning.

Opa's White Diamonds cologne scented the car, and her hair proved opry ready, teased high and sprayed stiff. Somewhere the country music angels were singing hallelujah. "Hello, Joe," she said. "I'm Opalina Wilson."

Opa never used her second husband's name. I liked to think it was because she never stopped loving my grandfather, but she said Opalina Wilson sounded a lot better than Opalina Thornhauser.

Joe gently shook her perfectly manicured hand.

I tried not to cringe. I wanted to tell him, *We're Panhandle women. We can take a firm handshake.*

"Hope you like big breakfasts, Joe," Opa said.

To my surprise, Joe and Opa talked the entire way to Amarillo about old country music stars. Apparently Joe knew everything there was to know about Johnny Cash—how the singer loved Bob Dylan's music, performed at Folsom Prison, and married June Carter. I couldn't have gotten a word in if I'd wanted to.

Calico County restaurant smelled of bacon and coffee. After we were seated, Joe said, "Rylee told me you recorded an album."

"Oh, that was a long time ago—1972; I cut it the year after arriving in Nashville."

Her album was a lot older than I'd realized. I did the math. Dad would have been about my age when Opa left.

"Were you born in Antler?" Joe asked her.

"Yes, I was, but I got away as soon as I could." She winked. "I'm glad to be back now. I can watch my granddaughters grow up. And Antler isn't a bad place to live. If you don't mind everyone knowing your business."

Stirring my hashed browns into my eggs, I thought about Dad and how he must have felt when Opa left. That would have been the same summer that Uncle Cal's brother, Wayne, died. It had been a tough summer for him.

I studied my grandmother, imagining the lines on her face disappearing, trying to picture her Mom's age. Mom and I didn't always get along. I didn't understand why things like tanning and working out every day meant so much to her. She was a good actress. Aside from her historical monologues, I'd seen her perform in a few church skits. She acted in summer stock one college break, and before I was born, she'd been in a few productions at the Amarillo Little Theatre. Maybe she had big dreams, but she would never leave us to chase them. Until now, I hadn't thought about my grandmother as someone who cared so much about her dream that she'd left her family behind to follow it.

When the waitress brought over our order, Joe devoured three scrambled eggs, chicken-fried steak, and biscuits and gravy. I wondered where he put it. He was as skinny as a Slim Jim beef stick.

"Are you sure you aren't from Texas?" Opa teased.

Joe burped. "Excuse me."

We laughed.

Then he said, "This is the first time I've ever had chicken-fried steak. One question, though."

"What's that?" I asked.

"Where's the chicken?"

∼

Opa paid the bill and dropped us off at the Amarillo Public Library downtown. It never failed. Every time I walked into this building, a tingle ran up and down my arms. Nothing smelled better than books, old and new. I wanted to bottle the scent. I couldn't wait until Antler's new library was finished.

Joe and I headed to the circulation desk to reserve computer time. Unfortunately, since it was Saturday, they were booked until noon, an hour before Opa was due to pick us up.

"Maybe your grandmother will wait," Joe said.

"She can't. She's got a show tonight and has to do sound checks with the band. Plus I have to work my shift."

"Are you going to ask me to go?"

"Where?"

"The opry," he said.

After his crack about the opry house on the tour, I'd never intended to invite him.

"The acts aren't exactly Johnny Cash." Then I asked, "Do you really want to go?"

He shrugged. "If I don't have anything better to do."

I changed the subject. "We're going to have to wait on the computer. So might as well see if a reference librarian can help us find that Florida town Sheriff Levi mentioned."

The reference librarians had helped me a ton when I was doing the Bill Monroe paper for Dad's class.

While I waited for the librarian to look up the info, Joe made his way to a cushy club chair near the magazines. He plopped down, not bothering to read. A moment later, he'd fallen asleep, and soft snores escaped his mouth. That big Texas-style breakfast had done him in.

The librarian wrote on a piece of notepaper and gave it to me. "Gibsonton, Florida," she said. "That's a fascinating place. I got caught up reading about it. The info I found said the town had relaxed codes so people could park trailers in the neighborhoods and elephants on the lawn. You're not running away to the circus, are you?"

She was smiling, so I knew she wasn't serious. "By the way, please tell your friend, no sleeping in the library."

I thanked her and joined Joe in the magazine section.

"Come on." I tapped him on the shoulder. "We can use a computer now."

At the keyboard, I typed "Zachary Beaver in Gibsonton, Florida."

Zero results.

"Bummer!" I muttered.

"Don't give up," Joe said. "We've learned something."

"What?"

"Zachary Beaver doesn't live in Gibsonton. Now look up his name in the White Pages."

I did what Joe suggested. Results: one hundred and twenty-seven Zachary Beavers. None of them lived in New York. They lived in California and New Hampshire. They lived in Utah and Maine. They lived all over the United States. Unfortunately long distance calling was expensive, and many of the listings didn't include phone numbers.

"It's a big world out there," I told him. Maybe this was a sign that we weren't supposed to find out what happened to Zachary. Dad's comment about why he didn't want to find him kept playing in my mind. I was ready to give up.

"Think like a detective," Joe said. "He doesn't live in Gibsonton, but he could live somewhere."

I scrolled down the list. "He could live anywhere."

"What else do we know?" Joe was clearly determined.

"He was in Antler the summer of 1971," I offered.

"Good thinking, Ambassador."

"We have a half hour left," I said. "Let's go upstairs to the microfilm area. Maybe we can find an article about his visit in an Amarillo paper. By the way, what topic are you doing for your history report?"

"It's a secret."

"Yeah, I'll bet." I wondered if he had plans to ever do it.

Upstairs we passed the children's section. A little boy was reading in the yellow claw-foot bathtub. I remembered doing that, too. We cut through the video section and made our way to the archives area.

I looked up Zachary Beaver's name in the 1971 Index for *Amarillo Globe-Times* and the *Amarillo Daily News*.

When we didn't find anything, Joe asked, "How about looking up *sideshow*?"

I ran my finger down the page and found one mention listed in July 1971 in the *Globe-Times*. The librarian stood behind the counter, lost in a book. After telling him the date we needed, he guided us to the microfilm machine and brought out a tiny box with a roll that looked like an old filmstrip. He demonstrated how to thread it through the reader and how to move the lever to the right, left, up, and down.

"Can I drive?" Joe asked. I stood, letting him take my seat. He moved the lever at such a quick speed, the articles turned into a black blur. When he reached

July, he slowed the projector. Then we saw the tiny article.

BIG VISITOR IN ANTLER

Sideshow boy billed as the Fattest Boy in the World made a stop in Antler, Texas. Paulie Rankin, the sideshow operator, said Antler was one of many destinations they will visit this summer. When asked how long they would stay in the bedroom community, Rankin said, "Long enough, but not long enough to wear out a pair of shoes."

That was it. No mention of Zachary's name.

"That stinks," Joe muttered, hitting the reverse lever.

We sat there silently watching the microfilm rewind and listening to its loud hum turn into a sputter as it reached the end of the strip.

"Well," I said, "now we know two things—he doesn't live in Gibsonton, Florida, and he was billed as the Fattest Boy in the World."

"I think we might be practicing deductive reasoning," Joe said.

I smiled. "Juan Leon would be proud."

"Where to now, Sherlock?" Joe asked.

I hadn't wanted to search for Zachary, and only agreed to make Joe happy. To me, it seemed like a lost cause, but Joe was enthusiastic. Finding Zachary seemed to mean a great deal to him. And it was nice having something to focus on together. I visualized a giant map of the United States with a trail dotted across every state. The possibilities were endless. Zachary Beaver could have gone anywhere. He could have gone everywhere.

"Let's retrace his steps after he left Antler," I said. "We could start by checking city newspapers from a nearby state. Maybe begin with Oklahoma."

We went downstairs to talk to the reference librarian.

～

When I got home, I heard our rickety washing machine clunking. Mom was making her way through a pile of towels, leisurely folding as she watched that old movie

An Officer and a Gentleman on TV. She must have seen it a dozen times.

I picked up a towel and joined her on the couch. "Mom, do you ever wish you'd gone to Hollywood?"

She broke her trance and looked at me like I'd asked if she'd ever thought about flying to Jupiter. Then she bent over and started to laugh. "What? Where did that come from?"

"Well," I said, "you were a theater major, and . . ."

She recovered, shook her head and stared back at the television. "No, but sometimes I wish I were Debra Winger. Boy, she can make me cry."

The movie came to the scene where Richard Gere marched into the factory and swept Debra Winger off her feet, carrying her out in his arms.

Mom sighed. "I just love this movie."

CHAPTER 28

At home I practiced the mandolin in my closet. If I squeezed in the back behind my clothes, and stacked bed and throw pillows against the door, the closet could be transformed into a tiny soundproof room.

Even though we hadn't found Zachary, it had been a great day. Joe hadn't seemed sad or angry. He'd almost seemed happy. We now had to wait until the next Saturday to see if the reference librarian had heard back from either the Oklahoma City or Tulsa library on what they may have found in their local newspaper archives from the 1970s. We'd only have to pay for copying and mailing charges. The librarian said it wouldn't cost more than a few dollars.

While I tried to play "Sweet Afton" by ear, I thought about Joe and the opry. He liked Opa and Johnny Cash.

I left my soundproof room and called him.

"If you don't have anything better to do, it's cowboy boots night."

"What?"

"If you wear your cowboy boots, you get in half price at the opry."

"I'd like to go, but I don't have any cowboy boots."

"Then you can go as my guest. That won't cost you a dime."

Mom and Mayzee were already at Opa's when Joe arrived at my house. We'd planned to walk to the opry together.

Dad looked at his watch. "You two go ahead without me. I'm waiting for Cal, as usual."

It was a slow night with only half the seats filled. I glanced around and saw Mrs. Wagner a few rows back, sitting with two friends. Twig hadn't attended since last summer. I wondered what she did now on Saturday nights. Dad and Uncle Cal made it to their seats right before the curtains rose.

Mayzee was the opening act. She sang "Candy Kisses" wearing a gigantic peppermint-striped bow in her hair. During an instrumental part of the song, she turned to the band and hollered, "Take it away, fellas!"

"Your sister cracks me up," Joe said.

"Thanks, I think."

"No, I mean it. She's good. At first I thought maybe your mom was a stage mom, but you can tell Mayzee wants to be up there."

He was right and wrong. Mayzee did love the stage, but Mom was a stage mom—just not the horrible kind you saw in movies. Sometimes I caught her on the sidelines mouthing the words.

Joe clapped loud for both of Mayzee's songs. Then when the headlining band came onstage, he seemed like a different person. He sulked low in his seat and didn't join in on the applause.

After the show, Dad and Uncle Cal invited us to join them at the Dairy Queen, but Joe wanted to go home.

People passed us by, heading either to their houses or cars. I couldn't hold back any longer.

"Well, you said you wanted to go. So you don't have to be so moody about it now."

He stopped walking. "I didn't mean to seem like I wasn't having fun. It's that my dad . . . my dad loved a lot of those songs."

I felt like an idiot. "I'm sorry."

"He'd sing 'I Walk the Line' around the house. Sometimes he'd belt out 'Welcome to My World' while he was in the shower. I had forgotten about that until now."

Not knowing what else to say, I asked, "Was he a good singer?"

Joe's face slowly slid into a grin. "Well, let's just say that he sang as good as your mom cooks meatloaf."

We laughed.

Joe shook his head. "He was terrible."

The cars on Highway 287 stopped at the corner traffic light, and we crossed the highway.

Joe continued. "I can't get used to this. Life happening without him. I keep hoping I'm going to walk into another room and never bump into anything that makes me think about him, but there is no other room. Everything reminds me of him. I think that's what moving here was about for my mom."

"Another room?"

"Yeah, but it's not working. She cries all the time. We still have a bunch of his stuff that she moved with us. She's hardly started to unpack, but she's emptied the boxes with his socks and shoes."

"I'm sorry," I told him. "If I'd known those songs would make you sad, I wouldn't have asked you to go."

"You didn't do anything wrong."

His words made me think of Twig and how she said I apologized too much. Sorry, I would always say. Squim.

We moved slowly down my street, passing the Bastrops' house. A light went off in a corner room, and I figured the elderly couple would soon be off to sleep.

There was a long space of quiet before Joe spoke again. "I'm mad because he isn't here tonight and won't be here tomorrow. Somebody at the memorial service told me that whenever we do think of him or remember something about him, in a way he is here. But it's not the same."

"No," I said. "How could it be?"

We walked the rest of the way in silence, and even though there was a big dose of sadness attached to the evening, something had changed between us. Maybe it started because of our search for Zachary Beaver. Whatever caused us to tumble into a friendship didn't matter. Joe had only been here a short time, and he was sharing his feelings with me. Not like Twig.

The night sky was clear except for the stars scattered high and low, like a big net, protecting us. It was one of the things I loved most about living in the Panhandle, one of the things I would miss if I ever left.

Joe and I arrived at my house, and he followed me to the door.

"Well, good night," he said.

"Good night." I slipped my key in the lock, but before I could turn it, Joe covered my hand with his. When I faced him, he circled his arms around my waist.

Then he cupped my face with his hands and lifted my chin until our lips were even, moving closer until they touched.

The kiss only lasted a second, but when it was over and Joe had walked away, I was still thinking about it.

CHAPTER 29

All I could think about was that kiss. I thought about
it every morning that following week when Joe met
up with Mayzee and me. I thought about it during
history class and at lunch. I could hardly talk to
Joe without tripping over my words, so I just stayed
quiet.

I wanted so badly to talk about it with someone.
But the someone I wanted to tell wasn't talking to me.
I wondered if Vernon had given Twig kiss number five. I
couldn't wait until Saturday when Joe and I would have

the Zachary Beaver Project to focus on and help me get my mind off that kiss.

Finally Saturday did arrive. We ate at Waffle House before heading to the Amarillo Public Library. The research librarian was away from her desk when Opa dropped us off, but there were two vacant seats in front of the computers.

Joe started typing.

"What are you doing?"

"Checking my email."

I sat there watching as he waited for his email box to appear. When it finally did and I saw Arham's name on five emails, I stood up. I didn't want to intrude.

"You don't have to go." Joe touched my wrist.

It's funny how a kiss made even a simple touch electrifying.

"Sit," he said.

I sat, but I focused on the reference desk while Joe read and laughed. He typed a quick message back.

"My mom won't let me call every night like I used to," he said. "It's too expensive. It's going to be hard to stay in touch until we get service."

"You can use the computer at Antler's library," I said, even though every time he mentioned Arham, I felt an imaginary tug-of-war—Arham on one side, me on the other, and Joe in the middle.

While I waited for the librarian to see if any Oklahoma articles had been discovered, Joe went to the computer catalogue to look up some books for his history report. He still hadn't shared his topic with me.

"How can I help you?" Then she smiled. "Oh, it's you—Rylee Wilson, right?"

I nodded.

"I have something for you."

She searched through a small stack of envelopes and pulled out one with my name on it. "It's a dollar fifty-three for postage."

I gave her the money, and she wrote out a receipt.

"So this is about a sideshow boy?"

"Yes." I was a little embarrassed, hoping she didn't think I was a gawker, the kind of kid who looked up weird things in the *Guinness Book of World Records*.

"Sounds interesting," the librarian said as she

handed over the package and receipt, smiling as if she'd given me a birthday present. Librarians must have to take an I-shall-not-judge oath.

I found Joe with two books, one about circus history and the other about a sideshow owner.

When I held up the package, he said, "All right!"

We were excited, making our way to a table in the corner of the reference area.

Inside the envelope, the pages were paper-clipped together. On top was a small article with the headline "Sideshow Act Visits Surrounding Towns." The article was short, but mentioned the acts included a teenager billed as the fattest boy in the world. We learned they visited Erick and Elk City, Oklahoma, before heading to the Oklahoma State Fair in Oklahoma City. I guess I'd hoped for more.

Joe must have read my face because he said, "Well, now we know where he went after Antler."

"And where he was in mid-September," I added.

The next page was a handwritten note from the librarian.

Joe read over my shoulder, "Ooh, *Ms. Wilson.*"

Dear Ms. Wilson,

I hope you don't mind, but I went beyond what you asked me to do because I remembered something from my childhood when a circus stopped in Kansas City with a sideshow boy like Zachary. So I asked my old college roommate who works at the Kansas City Public Library to do a little digging. I've attached the article she found. The article was dated March 21, 1973. Two years after his Antler visit. If I remember anything else, I'll let you know. I hope you find your Zachary Beaver alive and well.

BEATTY CIRCUS DERAILS NEAR KANSAS CITY

A train carrying a small circus company derailed outside of Kansas City last night. The Allen Circus Company was on their way to Saint Louis when the accident happened. Trapeze artists, elephants, chimpanzees, clowns, and sideshow acts were on board, including the fattest boy in the world. Two passengers died and seventeen were

injured. The owner of the small circus company,
H. R. Allen, said, "The show must go on." No
word was given if the circus would make their
way to Saint Louis. Names of the deceased and
injured are not being released at this time.

My stomach ached.

The whole time we were looking for him, even as far
back as first seeing him in Miss Myrtie Mae's photograph,
Zachary hadn't seemed real to me. He had been more
mythical and dreamlike than human. Until this minute.
Now it was as if I could reach out and almost touch him.
But was it too late? *Was Zachary Beaver dead?*

Joe pulled away a handwritten note paper-clipped
behind the article.

This note was from a Kansas City librarian.

*I was seven years old when this happened, and
I remember seeing the elephants and chimpanzees at the fairground. My mother told me
that they were housed there until some of the
circus people were released from the hospital.*

That's all I remember. I looked in the archives,
but couldn't find anything about the circus
employees who were injured or who died. I'm
so sorry, but I hope this helps some.

> Lois Maynard,
> Research Librarian
> Kansas City Public Library

I shook away the thought of what might be the worst outcome and added only the facts in my notebook:

1973
1. Zachary was with the Allen Circus.
2. He was on a train, heading to Saint Louis that derailed outside Kansas City.
3. He may have been killed or injured.

Joe and I kept reading the article and letters over and over. I wanted so much for Zachary Beaver to be alive. Now I was determined to find him as much as Joe. He had had enough death. I was thinking maybe we shouldn't go on, but just as I was about to suggest we stop our hunt, Joe said, "Zachary's got to be alive. I have a strong feeling he is. So where to next, Sherlock?"

I would have to ask the librarian to check the Saint Louis paper before we left, but we had an hour before Opa picked us up. We headed over to the periodical guides for the years 1973–75. They were books of indexes noting articles written on different subjects. I'd used them a lot to look up magazine articles on Bill Monroe.

"Look," Joe said, "here's an article in a *Newsweek* magazine about the Allen Circus."

Lucky for us, the Amarillo Public Library carried all the *Newsweek* magazines in their archives, and we were able to find the two full-page pictorial spread about the Allen Circus Company posing in front of the tent. There were the trapeze artists, a little man, an elephant, and a woman with some poodles standing on their hind legs. Then there, to the side of her, was a large man, a young man, maybe a teenager. My heart raced as I dragged my finger slowly under each name in the caption until I came to two words—*Zachary Beaver*.

Zachary Beaver had survived.

We held our palms up and slapped each other five.

Then Joe said, "Only twenty-six more years to go."

Fueled by what we'd learned, we blew through the rest of the 1970s editions with no luck, and we were disappointed when we didn't find anything in the 1980 edition either.

Our time for the day was up. We left the library clinging to a tiny sliver of hope hinged on one fact. Zachary Beaver had been alive in 1975.

CHAPTER 30

After we returned to Antler, I went to work at the stand. Usually the midday shift was busy, but that afternoon, Buster was the only customer I had in the first half hour. He proudly high-stepped toward the counter, holding a wilted bouquet of flowers wrapped in tissue paper. No telling how long he'd been carrying them around.

"It's my birthday, Rylee!" Then he smelled the flowers.

"Happy birthday, Buster! You get a snow cone on the house. What flavor?"

"That's a silly question."

"It is?"

"It's my birthday."

"I know. Do you want your usual—Coconut and Raspberry?"

"Buzzz! Wrong answer!" he said, holding up his palm.

"Oh, do you want Birthday Cake?"

"One hundred percent correct!"

"One Birthday Cake snow cone, coming up!" I said.

"Do I look different?" He held the bouquet up to his face and twisted in place.

Pretending not to notice the flowers, I leaned back and scanned Buster from head to toe. "Come to think of it, you look a whole year older."

He was older than me, but I wasn't sure of his age. I hoped he didn't want me to guess.

"No, that's not what I mean."

I checked again, rubbing my chin. "Oh! The flowers!"

"One hundred percent correct! I think the Mustangs gave it to me."

"I'll bet you're right."

But I knew it had probably been Mr. Pham. He loved giving flowers to people when they were sick or celebrating something. He'd delivered bouquets to nursing home residents, to Mom on the night of the school talent show, to Mayzee the first time she sang at the opry. Sometimes he surprised people on their birthdays. He was Antler's year-round Santa.

"Do you know what my birthday wish is?" Buster asked.

"A million dollars?"

"No. Guess again."

"Why don't you tell me?"

"I want a job at Wylie's Snow Cone Stand."

"You do?"

"Yep. So how about it, boss?"

"I'm not the boss, Buster. You need to ask my mom or dad."

"Can you ask them?"

"I can, but they'd be impressed if you did it."

"Okay. I'll ask on Memorial Day," he said.

"Buster, that's one of our busiest days."

He grinned. "I know."

When Buster walked away slowly, trying to carefully hold both his extra-large Birthday Cake snow cone and his bouquet of flowers, I realized there was a big possibility Mr. Pham had given flowers to someone moving to Antler, like the ones left on the Toscanis' doorstep. My head had been so clouded with the idea that the gift had something to do with romance that I had forgotten all about Mr. Pham, the mysterious flower giver.

Before Joe had to report for work, he dropped by the stand and plopped on the picnic table.

"I think I figured out who gave your mom the flowers," I said. "In fact, I'm certain that's who it was."

He jumped off the table like he was ready to fight his mother's secret admirer.

"Who?"

"Mr. Pham. I'm sure the bouquet was from him. I forgot how he always gives flowers for every occasion and never attaches a card."

"Random acts of kindness?"

"Maybe," I said, but I wondered if Mr. Pham may have felt like an outsider in Antler once, and the flowers were his way of making Joe's family feel welcome from the whole town. If they didn't know who gave them, they'd have to think it could be from anybody. And in a way that made them from everybody.

Joe nodded. "Makes sense. Now if only we could solve the Zachary Beaver mystery. I need to get off to work. I don't want Ferris to fire me."

"Ferris has never fired anyone."

Joe smiled. "He doesn't have to. They quit before he talks them to death."

As Joe made his way across the square, I remembered something that Ferris told me months ago. He'd said Zachary had a funny middle name. What if he'd started going by his middle name? It was a stretch, but it was still a possibility.

After my shift, I headed over to the Bowl-a-Rama Café. Twig wasn't there, but neither was anyone else. Seemed it was a slow day for snow cones and bowling. Ferris had found his audience, though. He sat on one of the benches in the bowling alley, talking to Joe.

I asked Ferris if he'd remembered Zachary's middle name.

He rubbed his whiskers. "Oh, what was that boy's

middle name? It was a singer, a famous singer's name . . ."

I started naming off Hank, Conway, Lester, Waylon, all the country and bluegrass names that came to mind.

And when I ran out, Joe offered up classic rock ones—Mick, Van, Dylan.

To each, Ferris said, "No, no, no."

"Oh, man," Joe said, "don't tell me it's Elvis."

"Elvis?" I repeated.

"That's it!" Ferris said. "Elvis. Oh, I'm glad I remembered that. I was getting concerned about my think box. But I guess it's as sound as a drum."

CHAPTER 31

At the library the next Saturday, we checked the late 1970s editions again, now using Elvis Beaver. A 1977 article listed Elvis Beaver's name in a Texas travel magazine. We headed to the archives desk, and the librarian fetched the issue with the article about a small circus that had to stay in East Texas for a month because a hurricane had hit Louisiana, their next planned stop. Inside the article was a quote:

240

"The good folks of Lindale have been very accommodating, but I'm partial to small Texas towns," circus spokesperson Elvis Beaver said.

"Look," I said, "he's a spokesperson. And I'll bet he's talking about Antler when he says he's partial to small Texas towns."

Searching for Zachary had become a treasure hunt. There were twenty-three more years to cover. We continued on, using the key words "Allen Circus," "Zachary Beaver," and "Elvis Beaver."

When the rest of the 1980s turned out a wash, I didn't say what I knew we were both thinking.

Then Joe called out, "Jackpot!"

Heads turned in our direction, but we didn't care. We were winning the game, with every move forward getting us closer to Zachary.

Joe found an Allen Circus mention in a 1990 issue of *Time* magazine. The article told about the closing of several small circuses in the last decade. The one Zachary worked for had performed for the last time. There was a quote from Elvis Beaver. "It's the end of an era. Now it seems only the biggest circuses are able to survive."

The 1991 periodical index had no Zachary or Elvis Beaver mention. Nor did the 1992 or '93 ones. It was as if Zachary had disappeared, as if he had died. We were so close. Now there was nothing.

Then Joe looked up from the 1994 edition and threw his fist the air. "Yes! Here's three mentions with Elvis Beaver."

The three articles were all from different state travel magazines, and Elvis Beaver was being credited as the writer. I thought back to the day we got the photograph and what Dad said about how Zachary loved reading travel books. It was like witnessing someone's dream coming true, Zachary's dream. He had become a writer.

Joe hurried to find 1995, and when he did, there were five articles by Elvis Beaver in more travel magazines. We gathered the remaining periodical guidebooks from 1996 to 1998. In every edition, we found references to more articles. He was a prolific writer. In 1998 alone, there were eleven articles, from "The Best Philly Steak

Sandwich in Pennsylvania" to "Jazz Clubs on New Orleans's Westbank."

Even though the library didn't carry the other magazines, we were convinced of two things.

1. Zachary Elvis Beaver was a writer.
2. He was alive and well three years ago.

Then I silently added to the list.

3. I've never seen Joe Toscani happier.

Before we had to meet Opa, Joe went to the bathroom, and I returned the editions to the shelf where I discovered the 1999, 2000, and 2001 volumes shelved in the late 1960s. Excited, I flipped through the pages of the 1999 edition, looking for Elvis Beaver, expecting to find at least a dozen articles.

But there weren't any. His name wasn't in the 2000 one either.

I turned to the 2001 edition and got the same results. I checked all the B's again, just in case, but there were no articles by a Zachary or an Elvis or even a Z. E. Beaver. A split second had changed everything. I couldn't help but believe my biggest fear might have come true.

I thought about not telling Joe. He had been so happy, but when he returned from the bathroom, he must have recognized the disappointment on my face.

"What's wrong?" he asked.

I hesitated, but then handed him the other indexes.

Joe read, running his finger down the list on the pages of each edition. Then he checked them again. He looked so sad that I forgot all about finding Zachary for Dad. Now I wanted him to be alive for Joe.

Then Joe slammed the last book shut, and we went outside to wait for Opa. "We should check the obituaries," he said. "Then at least we'd know. Nothing is worse than not knowing."

BOWL-A-RAMA CAFÉ

CHAPTER 32

Eight months had passed since the 9/11 attacks, and Dad said thousands of people whose family members died still hadn't received their loved ones' remains. Not an elbow or a rib or even a tooth to prove that they were truly gone. Joe's dad was among the lost.

I understood why Joe would need to know about his dad and why he thought it was best if we found out if Zachary was dead, too, but I didn't want to know. Because knowing meant I would have to carry that secret with me for the rest of my life.

～

Joe was scheduled to work Friday night, so I went to the Bowl-a-Rama Café to watch the ninepin bowling clubs. Unfortunately, that meant Vernon was working, too. The guys squatted on boxes in the pits behind the pins. After each frame, they jumped down and quickly returned the pins to their diamond pattern.

Antler was winning over White Deer. The teams only had two more frames left. I pretended to watch the rest of the game while noticing Joe's every move. Somehow he managed to look cute just by jumping off a box and resetting pins.

Ninepin was played long before tenpin. Ferris said it was outlawed during prohibition times because people were gambling on the games. One of the main things that made it different than tenpin was the scoring. The object in ninepin was to leave the middle pin, called the redhead (because it was painted pink or red), standing. When that happened, the team scored twelve points for a twelve-ringer. If a bowler knocked down all the pins, the team received nine points for a ringer. When I was on Antler's youth team, I managed to get a few ringers, but never a twelve-ringer.

Tonight Antler won, and the bowling teams left. I waited for Joe to finish his shift.

Vernon came out first and said, "Well, hello, hot stuff."

I ignored him.

Behind me, I heard a familiar voice say, "Hey."

Vernon's greeting wasn't meant for me. Twig stood only a few yards away. It felt strange. Outside of school, I hadn't breathed the same air as her in months.

Joe came over and said, "Hi, Twig."

My heart sank a little until he looked over at me, smiling so sweet, and said, "Hey, thanks for dropping by."

"I've got an idea," Vernon said. "Since no one else is here, how about a game of ninepin, only Twig and Rylee?"

Twig looked startled, but I knew her. She wouldn't back down on any dare. Then she said, "It's a team sport."

"You're a team, and she's a team," Vernon said. "Wagner against Wilson."

"I'm in," I said, instantly regretting it.

"Twig? Are you in?" Joe asked.

She nodded.

"All right!" Vernon hurried back to the box.

Joe spoke up. "I think you should set the pins for Rylee, and I'll do it for Twig."

"Don't trust me?" Vernon said in mock surprise.

"Nope," Joe said, "I don't."

Before returning to the pit, Joe came over to me and lowered his voice. "Just so you know, Twig's been practicing, and she's really good."

I ignored him, glancing over at Twig and asking her, "Are you sure you want to?"

"Whatever." She seized a pair of size-seven shoes from the shelf and slipped them on.

How could I feel scared and excited at the same time? I'd never taken the lead with Twig. Everything we did, everything we didn't do was always her idea.

Ferris came inside the bowling alley and stood at the back of the room. Mr. Pham joined him.

I took a big breath and said, "Go ahead."

Twig shook her head. "Nah, you go. I insist."

"After you," I told her.

"I'll flip a coin." Ferris dug in his pocket.

"Heads," Twig called out.

Ferris flipped the coin.

Tails. My decision.

"I'll go last," I said.

Twig went over and chose a ball, held it against her chest, and stared down the pins. She stepped up to the line, swung back her arm, and released the ball.

The ball rolled fast, straight down the middle until it hit the lead pin. Every pin followed. Ringer.

Vernon made a little victory cry—"Whoop, whoop, whoop"—while Joe quickly put the pins back in place.

Twig went again, and this time, seven pins fell.

At my turn, I focused on my secret weapon, the pin to the left of the lead one, closed my eyes for a split second, imagining the redhead standing alone. Then I took four steps toward the first line, and when I let go of the ball, it rolled its way to where I willed it. Every pin dropped except for the redhead.

"Twelve-ringer!" Joe yelled.

My first ever.

Joe jumped out of the pit and danced on the lane where the pins had once stood. All he needed were pom-poms.

Twig twisted her mouth. When she went up the next time, she dropped the ball a little too soon, and it jagged its way over toward the gutter.

"Focus!" Vernon yelled.

Her ball traveled the edge of the lane and dropped into the gutter right before reaching the pins.

My next frame, I bowled a ringer, then another.

Twig rolled a gutter ball and then another.

At the end of the third frame, Twig waved her hands over the air vent a long time before picking up the ball. She wasn't used to losing, especially to me, Soccer-ball Catcher Wilson.

"Aw, come on, Twig," Vernon said. "Concentrate, dingy!"

How could he call her that? Why would she put up with it? That wasn't like her at all. I wanted to punch Vernon. Instead I threw the ball, aiming and sending it straight to the gutter. Winning wasn't that important to me. Not like it was to Twig.

Twig looked over at me in bewilderment. Then she frowned. I hadn't fooled her. She knew I'd messed up on purpose.

Joe lowered his head from the pit and threw me a what-were-you-thinking look.

Then Twig picked up the ball and rolled a ringer.

Ferris and Mr. Pham turned and went back into the café. I wondered if they had a customer or if they were disappointed in me, too. Across the alley, Miss Myrtie Mae's picture of my dad and Uncle Cal on top of the roof hung on the wall. I stared at the photo, remembering all those last pictures she'd taken and how they'd made me realize so many of my decisions were based on Twig's happiness.

She was waiting now. So was everyone else.

I picked up the ball and eyed that left pin. And when I released the ball, it was so quiet, the rumble of it rolling down the lane was all that could be heard. I knew what would happen before it did. Every pin dropped except the redhead.

"Twelve-ringer!" Joe yelled.

Ferris and Mr. Pham were back.

The last two frames, Twig hit pins, but no ringers, no twelve-ringers, no points.

Frame five, I got a ringer. There was only one more

frame, and we already knew the outcome, but I rolled anyway. Ringer.

I won.

Mr. Pham nodded to me, and Ferris said, "Think I'll start calling you Twelve-ringer Rylee."

"Great game," Twig said. She was even kind of smiling. She was competitive, but only if she won it square and fair.

After saying good night to Ferris and Mr. Pham, Joe and I left the café. He held my hand and chattered about the game the whole way to my house.

"Man," he said, "I thought you were going to try and lose that game in the third frame."

I felt lighter than air, as if I could soar all the way home. It wasn't because Joe was holding my hand for the very first time or because I'd won the game. It was because something had shifted inside me when I realized it was okay to try and win.

When we reached my house, Joe said watching our game had mentally exhausted him, and he was going straight home to bed. "You were awesome tonight," he told me before leaning over and giving me a quick hug and a peck on my forehead. "I probably won't see you this weekend. I have to work on my history report."

I'd forgotten he hadn't done his and figured he'd probably forgotten, too.

"Mr. Wilson is a tough grader," I said. "Good luck."

"I'll need it."

"Just make sure you can back up your facts. That will impress him."

"One more thing," Joe said. "I was going to tell you later, but I'll tell you now. My mom and I are going home for a week. We leave a day before school lets out."

He called it home. New York was still home to him.

"When did you decide that?" I asked.

"This morning. Yesterday Mom found out they're ending the cleanup at Ground Zero, and they're doing a ceremony for the unrecovered dead." His voice cracked on the last word. Then he raised his chin as if to get a grip on his emotions. "We're going to be in the honor guard. If you want to watch, it will be on television."

"Of course I'll be watching," I said.

"Don't expect me to wave or anything."

We laughed a little, then he walked backward from

my front porch until he reached the road, gazing at me the whole way.

~

The next morning I slept until nine, later than I ever remembered. It felt strange to greet the sun instead of the moon. Once out of bed, I opened my windows, took my mandolin out of the closet, and began to play "Sweet Afton." My rendition proved mediocre at best. I still struggled with the bar chords on the chorus, but it felt good to play and release a part of myself into the world instead of hiding behind the clothes and pillows inside my closet.

When I finished the song, I went downstairs, where my family sat at the breakfast table. The three of them gazed at me with silly grins while I settled in my chair and struggled to untie one of Mayzee's tightly knotted napkins.

Then Mayzee asked, "Would you play 'You Are My Sunshine' for me at the opry?"

We Remember
9-11-01

CHAPTER 33

Sunday morning I looked out the window toward Joe's bedroom. I'd gotten in the habit of checking it ever since that day weeks ago when I saw him waiting for Uncle Cal. After that, the lamp was never on before dawn.

Until now.

I watched for a moment, and when I didn't see any moving shadows, I looked down at the street, but Joe wasn't there. Then I rushed to my north window and waited for Uncle Cal, expecting him to make his appearance. Maybe I should have told him that Joe might have changed his mind.

After a while, I gave up and listened to my iPod. I was great at playing the air-mandolin, my fingers mastering G-sharp minor. If only my actual daily afternoon sessions did it justice. But I was getting better even if the improvement was slow going. At least I was prepared to play "You Are My Sunshine" for Mayzee in a couple of weeks.

One song later, I glanced out my window again. There they were, Uncle Cal and Joe, side by side, coming in from the west, returning from a neighborhood ride. When they got to Uncle Cal's driveway, they lifted their palms and slapped each other five. Then Joe rode on, turned at the corner, and cycled the rest of the way home.

~

Joe was wearing his FDNY T-shirt. He looked nervous. Remembering the books he'd checked out of the library, I wondered if his report was on a sideshow operator or a circus owner. I just hoped he didn't mention anything about Zachary Beaver.

After taking attendance in history, Dad said, "We have one last report to hear. Mr. Toscani?"

Joe opened his folder and pulled out the pages.

Then with hands shaking, he began to read.

"If it hadn't been for the firefighters of the twentieth century, many United States cities would have lost more lives, homes, and businesses."

His voice cracked a little, and a few sentences in, he stopped reading. I glanced around the class, but everyone was sitting politely waiting. By now the word had spread through town about Joe's dad.

Joe started reading again, covering the heroic acts of both the volunteer departments and full-time firefighters. We listened to him talk about the ongoing training the firefighters had so they could handle all kinds of fires from high-rise buildings to confined areas. He shared how they had to have an extensive education and skill in fighting wildland fires and working around hazardous materials.

Ending his report, he said, "When a person becomes

a firefighter, they've made a decision that could come at a high cost. When they leave the front doors of their homes each day, they never know if that will be the last time they will see their families. It was true in the last century, true in this century, too."

Dad cleared his throat. "Thank you, Joe. That was excellent. Any questions for Joe?"

Even though Dad always invited the class to ask questions after everyone's report, I wished he could have made an exception with Joe. He knew how the Jerks behaved in this class. When Vernon's hand went up, I was wishing Dad had used some deductive reasoning.

"Mr. Clifton?" Dad's tone had a load of reluctance pinned to it.

"Joe, how long was your dad a fireman?" Vernon asked.

Joe raised his chin. "Twenty-one years."

I hoped Vernon wasn't going to start bragging about how his dad was a volunteer fireman and had served for years, too.

Instead Vernon asked, "What was his name?"

"Frank Toscani," Joe said, sliding into his seat, his back now to the class.

"You must really be proud of what he did. I mean your dad, Frank Toscani, was a hero." Vernon scooted his chair away from his desk, stood up, and began to clap.

Boone followed his lead. So did Twig, Juan Leon, and Frederica. Now everyone was on their feet, clapping, including Dad and me.

Then Vernon hollered, "FDNY!" And the rest of us joined in. "FDNY! FDNY!"

There was no stopping us. We clapped and clapped, and when Mr. Arlo stuck his head in the classroom to see what was going on, we continued to clap.

None of us had lost a parent in that tragedy, nor seen firsthand the horror of the towers collapsing. We had only witnessed it through our television screens and believed that it was real. It wasn't enough to fly our flags, gather in prayer circles, paint a café in patriotic colors, or send our dollars to help rebuild.

But we had to do something.

Joe just sat there in his front row seat, staring down at his desk, his shoulders raised to his ears. His face was hidden, but if I could have seen his eyes, I knew what I would have found there. I leaned over, touched his arm, and motioned for him to turn around.

He quickly wiped his eyes with his sleeve. Then he looked back at us, taking in all of the best that our seventh-grade history class could give.

ANTLER
PUBLIC LIBRARY
HOURS
TUES.-THUR.-FRI. 1:PM ʈᵒ 4:PM.

CHAPTER 34

The day before the school year ended, Joe and his mom left for New York. They would spend a few days with his aunt and uncle in his old neighborhood before the ceremony on May 30. I tried not to think about him having fun with Arham, going to all the places they used to go, like Owl Head's Park, or having an egg cream at Hinsch's.

The first official day of summer vacation, I pedaled

to the edge of town where they were building the frame of the new library. The sounds of saws singing and nail guns popping filled the air. Dad said the rest of the construction would go faster now. Usually that would be exciting, but nothing seemed worth celebrating.

Deep in thought, I rode away from the worksite and somehow ended up at the courthouse basement door, in front of the Antler Public Library sign. The library would be closed soon to prepare for the move across town. I wanted to take a last look around.

"Hello." The voice came from somewhere behind the stacks of boxes and books. A tall young woman with blond curly hair and a cheerful face emerged from the spot where the checkout counter used to be.

"Hi," I answered. "I'm sorry. I didn't know anyone would be here."

"Can I help you?" Her voice was as friendly as her face, almost as if it were suppressing giggles.

"I used to come here all the time."

"Come back for a last look?"

"Yes, I guess." My timing was late. I wished I'd visited sooner. "Are you the new librarian?"

"I sure am. My name is Kennedy Parsons."

"I'm Rylee Wilson." I held out my hand, and she gave it a nice firm shake.

"My dad didn't tell me you'd started. You may have met him. He's on the building committee. His name is Toby Wilson."

She nodded. "Oh, yes, Mr. Wilson. He interviewed me first."

"Are you from the Panhandle?"

"Yes, I'm from Borger."

That explained the good firm handshake.

"So it's not so different there," she said. "Well, bigger for sure."

"For sure," I said. Then we both laughed.

"But I've driven through Antler lots of times, and I always thought it was a cute town. So charming—like the opry house."

"That's my grandmother's. Opalina Wilson."

"Oh, I love that!"

"Do you like country music?"

"Well . . . ," she said, "I'm a bit of an indie rock fan. Sorry."

Twig was going to love knowing that.

"But I've already had the best bowl of pho here that I've ever eaten."

"At the Bowl-a-Rama Café?"

"Yes, I met Ferris and Mr. Pham. I'm going to enjoy living here."

I thought about how Kennedy's first impression of Antler was a lot different than Joe's. Maybe some people were meant for small towns. And some people weren't.

"Have a look around if you like," she said. "I'm taking inventory so I can know what to order."

"Thanks." I took in the space, gazing over to the spot where I used to sit when I wanted to get away and escape in a book. Even though I hadn't spent much time here in the last couple of years, I was going to miss this place.

"Let me know if there's anything I can help you with. Although you've spent a lot more time here than me. I may have to ask *you* a question."

"Can we still dial up the Internet?" I asked.

"Sure, changing the service will be one of the last things we do. Would you like to use it?"

As I made my way to the computer, she said, "We'll have three computers in the new library. Miss Myrtie Mae Pruitt was a generous woman."

I settled in front of the computer, entering my account number and password. Even though I had closed the door on the search, I found myself typing the words *Zachary Beaver*. After his name, I slowly typed *obituary*. My finger hovered over the enter button, but I couldn't do it. I hit the back key and removed the word, one letter at a time. Then I deleted his name and started over.

There were well over a hundred Zachary Beavers in the United States, but this time I searched for "Zachary Elvis Beaver" in the White Pages. Results: zero.

Then I tried "Zachary E. Beaver."

Results: four.

The entries included their approximate ages. I didn't know how old Zachary was, but I figured he was about Dad's age. Dad would turn forty-four in a couple of weeks. There was only one Zachary E. Beaver identified in his forties—age forty-six, living in Tampa, Florida.

And there was a phone number.

I stared at it. My heart felt like it was running the fifty-yard dash. Why hadn't we thought of searching for him in the White Pages again after we'd learned his middle name? It would have been so easy.

I scribbled the number down on a notepad, thanked Kennedy, and started to leave. Then I turned and said, "Welcome to Antler!"

Welcome to
ANTLER
IF YOU DON'T WANT SOMETHING TOLD,
DON'T TELL US!
POPULATION 856   ELEVATION 3,600

CHAPTER 35

I wanted to rush home and make the call, but I had to report for snow-cone duty. Finding out if the Zachary E. Beaver living in Tampa, Florida, was our Zachary would have to wait until after my shift. If it didn't turn out to be him, I'd close the door on the search forever.

It was so hot, the kind of afternoon that usually created long lines for a snow cone, but there was only one person who showed during my first hour.

Twig stepped up to the counter.

"Where's your friend?" I asked. "I mean, your boyfriend."

"Vernon's not my boyfriend," she said. "He was never my boyfriend."

I shrugged. "The usual?"

Twig had been growing her hair out for a while now, and she started twirling a short lock, glancing around the square as if she wanted to be rescued. She wasn't used to seeing me act indifferent. I wasn't used to it either, and after feeling a split second of satisfaction, I decided I didn't like it.

"The usual?" I repeated.

She nodded. "When's Joe getting back?"

"On June first." I kept drizzling the Lemon Tang syrup over the ice.

"Whoa," she said. "That's enough."

I handed the snow cone to her.

Twig continued, "Mrs. Toscani gasses up at Allsup's once a week. Mom told her she'd always wanted to be a nurse, and Mrs. Toscani told Mom she should enroll in school. Now Mom is going to start taking classes at Amarillo College this summer."

I couldn't stand holding my feelings back. I liked Twig's mom. "That's really great," I told her. "She'll be a terrific nurse."

"Thanks," Twig said. When I didn't say anything else, she bit her lip.

"Yeah, it's really great," I repeated.

"She's never been happier." Twig rolled her straw paper against the counter, turning it into a tiny ball. "I kind of don't know how to act without all the arguing in the house."

So much had happened between us, but I really wanted to know how things were for her since the divorce.

"How's your dad?" I asked.

Stabbing the ice with her straw, she said, "Still ticked. What do you expect? I see him once a week, though."

Then she pulled out her wallet, but I held up my palm.

"On the house."

She nodded and then slipped a folded dollar bill in the tip jar. "You know," she said before walking away, "sometimes I used to wish your parents were mine."

It was a weird thing to say. I didn't understand until later, when my shift was ending and I saw my parents walking toward the stand, holding hands. To me, Twig had everything—looks, confidence, and talent, but I guess I always had something that she never had.

I gathered my tips, all coins, except for Twig's dollar bill folded nice and neat. When I undid it, a piece of paper slipped out. On it was one word: *Squim*.

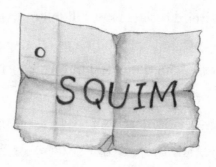

CHAPTER 36

Squim. Twig had apologized. I stared at that piece of paper a long time, wanting to think about what the next step would be, but my shift had ended and my mind needed to be on one thing—Zachary Beaver.

Once home, I went to my room and dragged my phone to my bed, trying to forget about Twig for the moment.

I dialed the Tampa number, figuring that if this wasn't the right Zachary, I'd have a lot of explaining to do when the phone bill arrived. Even if it was, I'd have a lot to explain.

While the phone rang, a knot formed in my gut. By the fourth ring, I decided this was a dumb idea. But I let the phone ring two more times.

After the sixth ring, I started to hang up.

Before I did, I heard "Hello? Hell—ooo?"

"Is this Mr. Beaver?"

"What are you selling?" He had a New York accent similar to Joe's.

I started backward with the info we'd found. "Is this Zachary Beaver who writes travel magazine articles and used to be a spokesperson for the Allen Circus?"

"What's this about?"

I'd come too far, so I continued. "The Mr. Beaver who was in a train wreck?"

"What the—"

"Is this the Zachary Beaver who was in Antler, Texas, the summer of 1971?"

A long pause followed.

I waited, but he didn't speak. Before he could hang

up, I blurted, "My name is Rylee Wilson, and my dad is Toby. Do you remember him?"

"Is this a joke?"

"No, sir, I've been trying to find you."

"Toby Wilson, Antler, Texas, summer of 1971? Yes, Rylee, I remember him well."

CHAPTER 37

"You're really Toby Wilson's daughter?"

My heart raced, but then the thought entered my mind that maybe this wasn't our Zachary. That he was just some guy with the same name who was fed up with unsolicited calls and was playing a trick on me. He hadn't offered me any information yet that proved he was the Zachary I was looking for. And I'd just blurted out every detail I knew about him.

"That town hasn't blown away?" he asked.

"Antler is still here." I wanted it to be him, but now I was skeptical. He could be talking about any little town.

"That guy, Ferris, is he still there too?"

This *was* Zachary! "Yes, sir!"

"Is he still a big yapper?"

"Yes, sir."

"Well, some things never change." Then his voice softened. "Is everything okay with Toby?"

"Oh, yes, sir. He's fine. He doesn't even know I'm doing this."

"Oh?"

"I wanted . . . um, I mean, I needed to find out—"

"Wanted to make sure I was still breathing and upright, huh?"

"Oh, well, um." I cleared my throat.

"That's okay, I understand. So how the heck are the boys?"

"The boys?"

"Toby and Cal."

"They're fine. Dad is a teacher, and Uncle Cal works on the cotton farm."

"Uncle Cal? Did your dad marry Kate?"

"Oh no, sir. We just call him uncle."

"Oh, that's good. How is Kate?"

"She's fine. She lives in New York."

"Married, is she?"

"No, she's not married."

"Really?" He almost squeaked the word. "That's nice. Has she got a special guy?"

"I don't think so, but I don't really know." Why did he seem so interested in Kate?

"So who is your mom? That pretty little blond your dad had a huge crush on? What was her name?"

"Tara."

"No," he said. "I think that was her bratty little sister. But you're close. It had something to do with *Gone with the Wind*. Scarlett! That was her name."

"No, he's not married to her." I decided not to explain that the bratty little sister was Mom.

"Well, you can't have everything. I'm sorry. I'm sure your mom is a lot prettier than Scarlett."

I glanced at the clock. I was pretty sure long-distance phone calls cost more in the middle of the day, so I needed to get to the point quickly.

"Mr. Beaver, my dad's birthday is in a couple of weeks. Do you think you could call and surprise him?"

"Nah, I don't think that would be possible." His voice was serious, even a little annoyed.

"Oh, I see." But I really didn't. Finding Zachary hadn't been easy. There were so many times when we could have stopped searching.

"Kid, I'm just joking with you. What's the number?"

Innis's
DRUG
STORE

Original Soda
Fountain Inside

CHAPTER 38

I wanted Joe to be the first person I told about finding Zachary, but I ended up telling Mom. She needed
to know about the phone call, the long-distance one I
made, and the surprise call from Zachary that would
happen on Dad's birthday.

Mom wasn't upset with me about the call or searching for him. She practically did a cheer. "I thought you
and your dad were cut from the same cloth, but I guess
you have a little of me in you after all."

I told her I'd never have started to search for Zachary if it weren't for Joe.

Mom said getting a surprise call from Zachary would be Dad's best birthday gift. She asked for his number, just in case Zachary forgot. If he did, she'd sneak away from the party to give him a reminder call.

"Just don't tell your little sister," she said, "or Cal."

Then she shocked me by walking over to Zachary's picture in the corner of the room and positioning it over the mantel.

∾

The morning of May 30, my parents decided to open the snow cone stand late so our family could watch the Ground Zero Ceremony. The honor guard was made up of family members of the dead, the NY Fire and Police Departments, and other volunteer and emergency workers. Joe had said he and his mom would be holding framed pictures of his dad as they walked. I noticed some of the other families did, too. Some of the firemen had photos tucked under the bands of their helmets.

Bells rang for all the firefighters who died. Then an

empty coffin draped with an American flag, representing those who were never recovered, was carried to an ambulance.

The last steel beam was placed on a flatbed truck also covered with the flag. The bands played "America the Beautiful" and Taps. NYPD helicopters flew overhead in honor of the dead.

The whole time, I thought about Joe. And even though I couldn't see him in that huge honor guard crowd, I felt like I was standing right next to him, watching the ambulance carrying the empty coffin drive away.

CHAPTER 39

The Toscanis returned on June 1, and Joe was at my house first thing the next morning. I was glad to see him, relieved that he came back.

"Want to ride?" he asked.

I couldn't wait to tell him about finding Zachary. I followed him down the street on my bike until we were riding side by side. Skipping Gossimer Pit, we crossed the highway and then the railroad tracks.

We were almost at Juan Garcia's home place when we stopped.

"I have to tell you something," Joe said. He sounded so serious. Telling him about Zachary would have to wait.

The wind kicked up, and my hair stuck to my lip gloss.

He leaned over his handlebars and gently pulled a strand away from my mouth and tucked it behind my ear.

"I lied to you about not knowing how to ride."

I laughed. "I kind of figured that out already. Either that or you're the fastest learner I've ever met."

"Can we rest here for a minute?" Joe asked.

He got off his bike, and I did the same. We walked our bikes along the track, and Joe told me about how his dad bought him a bicycle a few months before he died.

"It was an expensive bike, and I know it cost him a lot of money. I loved it. I rode everywhere around our neighborhood, to Owl's Head Park, to Fort Hamilton and the Verrazzano Bridge. There was always this guy riding his beat-up bike around the bridge. I think he might have been homeless. Whenever he saw me, he'd say, 'Man, I like your wheels.'

"One night I left the bike out near our stoop and my dad brought it in when he came home, warning me that it was going to get stolen. I messed up. A week later, I forgot and left it out another night. When he got home from work, Dad happened on a couple of kids trying to take it. But when they saw him, they took off. I wasn't allowed to ride my bike for two weeks."

Joe got quiet, and we stopped walking. His nose twitched, and he swiped it with the back of his hand. I wondered if the Ground Zero Ceremony had unlocked something, made him want to unload, and that was why he was telling me all of this now. Because even though he'd told me about what had happened to his dad, there was always this feeling that he was holding back.

He took a deep breath as if to steady his nerves and continued talking. "Whenever some big fire incident happened in Manhattan, one that would make the news, my dad would always call us as soon as he could to let us know he was okay. On 9/11, I was in school when I learned about the towers being hit. I had a feeling, a strong feeling that he was there. Mom did too.

She came and got me an hour later and took me home. Hours passed with no word, and we knew.

"By three o'clock, I couldn't stand being inside the apartment any longer. I jumped on my bike and road out of Bay Ridge and all the way to the Brooklyn Bridge. I knew the towers were gone, but I couldn't have seen them if I'd wanted. Across the East River, the smoke blotted out the view. It took over the sky. The bridge was thick with people. They were pouring off that bridge from the other side because they couldn't get a taxi or ride the subway. Some were crying, men and women. Most of them were walking in a daze. I had to get to the other side, but a cop stopped me. He told me I should go home. He said 'should,' but it sounded like an order. I almost crossed anyway, but I would have been a salmon going upstream. Maybe I was scared, too. Scared to find out the worst. So I rode back home.

"When I got there, my aunt and uncle were at our apartment, and Mom was crying. My uncle had been on a sales call near the towers. He kept talking to people, trying to find his way to some of Dad's coworkers. He found out that Dad went in a second time, right before the building collapsed.

"He was gone."

Joe's hands had turned into tight fists.

"Later a lady told us my dad saved her life, carried her down three flights of stairs of the second tower. I wish he hadn't gone back in. That night, I left my bike out, this time on purpose. I figured it would surely be gone by morning. I wanted so badly for my dad to be walking in with it, yelling at me, telling me I was grounded for six months. But in the morning the bike was there and my dad wasn't.

"Friends and neighbors started coming by with food as if we'd had a funeral. I tried to call Arham, because we'd heard his dad was gone too. But I couldn't get through. I escaped on my bike and rode to the Verrazzano Bridge. When I saw that guy riding his old beat-up one, I hollered to him, 'Hey, how would like these wheels?'

"I got off my bike, left it on the ground, and walked home."

My throat felt like it was stuffed with cotton balls. I

reached over and touched his arm. "I'm so sorry about your dad. I really am, Joe."

His eyes were wet, but he wasn't finished. "My mom couldn't handle being in our apartment without him like I couldn't handle seeing that bike. That's why she was ready to escape. When the house here hadn't sold, she thought it was a sign."

The train was coming from the east, getting louder the closer it got, but we stayed near the tracks.

Ka-nuck, ka-nuck.

"But this isn't home," Joe said. "It never will be. And since we went back last week, Mom knows that, too."

My gut began to hurt.

Ka-nuck-ka-nuck.

Even though the train swallowed his words, I heard them loud and clear.

"We're going back, Rylee," Joe said. "We're going back home."

I stared at the train cars rushing by. I stared at the Engelmann daisies, their long stems whipping to and fro. I stared everywhere except at Joe.

My head pounded, and I felt like someone had squeezed the breath out of me.

These last few months, I'd hoped Joe and his mom would stay, but part of me knew they wouldn't. It wasn't just the still-packed boxes and Mrs. Toscani not beginning her job search. It was because every time Joe spoke about Bay Ridge, it reminded me of how I felt about Antler.

Maybe that was the hardest part, because I'd let myself get close to him, even when deep down I suspected he wouldn't be here for long. I'd been like someone wading into the deep end of the ocean who didn't know how to swim.

The wind howled, and I gazed at the water tower bearing our town's name. Joe was still staring down the track, although the train had long since passed.

My eyes filled.

Joe turned, and this time he reached out to me. "You've been the best part of this, Rylee. I'm going to miss you so much."

I couldn't talk or move.

He dropped his arms to his side. "Are you okay?"

"I am. I promise. Here, I'll prove it." I held out my hand. "Shake."

He took hold, but shook it gently.

I pulled it away and then held it out once more. "Again," I said. "Panhandle women are tougher than they look."

He grabbed hold, and this time he gave my hand a nice firm shake.

My whole body felt numb, and I had a big lump in my throat, but managed to say, "Good job."

For the longest time, Joe wouldn't let go. Before he finally did, he lifted my hand to his lips and kissed it. I wanted to freeze the moment, keep us this way forever, standing somewhere between Juan Garcia's home place and the Antler railroad crossing. But I knew he was right. He had to return to New York. He had to go back home.

I didn't tell him about finding Zachary. That could wait for another day. Instead, we got on our bikes and rode to Gossimer Pit, then rounded the square. Then we decided to cross the highway again. The sun had begun to set in the western sky, a peachy glow resting on the horizon. We pedaled slowly by the tracks like we weren't in any hurry. But when the last train of the day neared, we increased our speed, riding alongside it with our arms stretched high in the air.

CHAPTER 40

A couple of days after Joe told me they were leaving, a
FOR SALE sign went up in his yard. Whether they sold the
house or not, they would leave before the end of June.
It happened so quickly, almost as if Joe being here
hadn't happened at all, like catching a snowflake that
melted instantly in your palm. Before it was caught,
that flake could have turned into anything, a snowball,
an igloo, or just magical frost on a window. But then
it was gone.

~

It would have been enough to keep me moping, but the next day was Dad's birthday, and I was excited about the surprise phone call from Zachary.

Dad never liked a fuss made over his birthday. All he claimed he wanted was Mom's red velvet cake and his three girls and Opa. He had no idea, but this year would be different. Uncle Cal would be there. So would Joe and his mom. Which was a good thing, because I knew Joe didn't want to miss out on Zachary's surprise.

When I told Joe about finding Zachary, he'd said, "Knew it!"

I asked if he would have tried to search for Zachary on his own if I hadn't.

"Probably not. Zachary was really yours to find."

"I would never have tried to find him if it hadn't been for you."

Joe shrugged it off, but I believed even if we never saw each other again after he left Antler, searching for and finding Zachary Beaver was something we'd done together.

Friday night, Mom said she'd make meatloaf, but

Opa convinced Mom she had enough to do and Opa told her she'd make a big pot of chili. So at least Dad would have a decent meal for his birthday.

Joe and his mom had only been at Dad's birthday party a moment before Mayzee spilled the beans about our upcoming performance at the opry Saturday night.

"What?" Joe was surprised. "You play the mandolin? How did I not know this?"

"I'm learning," I told him. "Opa is teaching me."

"And she's pretty darn good," Opa said. "It runs in the family. And she's humble. I don't know where she gets that from, though."

"Is it tomorrow night?" Joe asked.

I nodded.

"Cal and I are going for a long ride that day, but we're starting out early. I promise I'll be there."

Joe must have been talking about riding to the canyon overlook. I was glad he was finally going.

Dinner started off quiet until Uncle Cal told a corny joke. At least it was clean. Then everyone seemed to chatter at once.

Dad opened Mom's gift first, and when he saw the

camera, he asked, "Is this what I think it is? Miss Myrtie Mae's?"

"Yes," Mom told him. "When you didn't buy it, you made my birthday shopping easier."

Dad started to laugh. "I was wondering about that charge from the auction house."

He kept examining it, turning the camera every which way. "I'd like to donate this to the new library. They could display it in the showcase at the entry."

"Dad," I said, "maybe everyone who received Mrs. Myrtie Mae's pictures could loan them for the opening."

"Smart thinking, Rylee," Dad said. "That would be a nice tribute."

I glanced at the clock. It was five minutes until 6 P.M. Zachary was due to call at 6:05. So I handed Dad the scrapbook I'd put together. "Here, Dad. Happy birthday!"

Dad opened it and read the first page. *The Zachary Beaver Project*. He gave me a perplexed look.

Uncle Cal leaned in.

"Turn the page," Mayzee demanded.

"So this was what you were doing in the library," Opa said.

On the next page was a copy of the first article we found about Zachary coming to Antler. Each page of the journey was revealed—the Oklahoma towns, the Allen Circus train derailing in Kansas City, the Louisiana hurricane. The article in *Time* magazine about the closing of the Allen Circus. Judging from Dad's face, he must have thought the following pages were going to be dismal, as if he was expecting to see Zachary's obituary. Instead, he read off the titles of the articles Zachary wrote.

I looked at the clock. It was seven after six, and the phone hadn't rung.

Two minutes late wasn't a big deal, but then three more minutes passed, and Zachary was officially late. I glanced over at Mom, but she hunched over Dad's shoulders reading the article titles aloud.

"Mom," I said, "can I see you in the kitchen, please?"

"In a minute." She didn't even glance up.

Joe twisted up a corner of his mouth and slightly shrugged.

Mom kept admiring the scrapbook. She wouldn't even look my way.

I got up from the table and started toward the stairs to make the call to Zachary myself.

The doorbell rang when I reached the hall.

"Rylee," Mom hollered, "please get the door."

"I'll get it!" Mayzee rushed past and beat me to it.

In the doorway stood a large man with salt and pepper hair, wearing suspenders and holding a cane.

"Hello, Zachary Beaver!" yelled Mayzee.

CHAPTER 41

Although Zachary Beaver was large, he was a lot smaller than his younger self portrayed in Miss Myrtie Mae's picture. He told us he'd lost a lot of weight years ago after the train accident and even had to wear a fat suit when he still traveled as a sideshow act.

"The accident left me with this limp," Zachary said, "but it's got its fringe benefits. Even ladies give up their seats for me on the bus."

I wouldn't have recognized him and wondered how Mayzee did. It had been thirty years since that picture was taken. Mayzee confessed she'd heard Mom talking to Zachary on the phone, inviting him to Dad's birthday party. No one knew she knew that he was flying into Amarillo. It was the biggest secret she'd almost kept.

For a few moments, Dad was in shock. Even Uncle Cal was speechless for a minute or two.

"So you're not going to ask one of your nosy questions like where I go to the bathroom?" Zachary asked Cal. "Speaking of, where is the john?"

After he returned to the table, the three of them started reminiscing about the good ol' days when there really was a Wylie Womack and a Dairy Maid instead of a Dairy Queen. They seemed to be talking all at once. Sometimes Joe or Mom would ask questions. I kept quiet, though, looking around the table at the happy faces, listening to the stories and the laughter, witnessing proof that even old friends could come together again.

Zachary told us he was writing a memoir about his life as a sideshow boy. He'd stopped writing travel articles for the last couple of years so that he could finish it. The book was due out next month.

After the party, Joe and I went with Dad, Uncle Cal, and Zachary to Gossimer Pit. No one was riding bikes there, but tire tracks covered the entire area.

"It's hard to believe I almost drowned here," Zachary said.

"You mean when we baptized you?" Dad asked.

"Yeah, Toby," Uncle Cal said. "Don't you remember when we almost dropped him?"

Zachary snorted. "Just think, if that had happened, I would never have left Antler. And after the lake dried up, kids would have been cycling over my bones to this day."

～

If someone had told me a few weeks ago that I'd be playing my mandolin in front of Zachary Beaver, I wouldn't have believed them. By the time the opry house doors opened the next day, Zachary and Dad had eaten lunch at the Bowl-a-Rama Café (entertained by Ferris's stories) and covered all of Antler's stomping grounds.

Twenty minutes before Opa went onstage, the band was warming up and Mayzee and I were sitting in the greenroom waiting for our cue to go on. We heard a knock on the door and Zachary's voice: "Are you decent?"

"Yes, sir," I called out.

Zachary slowly opened the door. He was wearing a cowboy hat and cowboy boots.

"Rylee, I just wanted to tell you to break a leg or whatever they say in cow town."

Mayzee sprang to her feet. "How about me?"

"Of course, you little prairie dog. You go ahead and break a leg, too. Break two legs, if you like."

He turned his attention back to me. His hands rested on his cane, and he cleared his voice. "I wanted to thank you for finding me, Rylee. Your mom told me all the trouble you and Joe went through. I've thought of your dad and Cal a lot over the years. Figured they'd forgotten me. I guess that's why I never reached out. But true friendship never fades, no matter what happens. So thanks for teaching me that."

I thought of Twig, but said, "I'm glad you've met up again. Thanks for making Dad's birthday really special."

Zachary tipped his hat as he backed out of the room, closing the door behind him.

A few seconds later, Opa entered with a bouquet. She smiled, handing it to me. "It looks like you have a fan."

I could tell right off that the flowers weren't from Mr. Pham. These weren't any florist or grocery-store-type flowers. These were Engelmann daisies. I pulled out the card that was tucked between the stems and read,

Sorry about the weeds, but I wanted you to have something for your special night.
Break a leg!
Joe

Mayzee and I were the second act to perform. I was grateful for that because my fingers felt jittery knowing that Zachary and Joe were out there in the audience.

"Are you nervous?" I asked Mayzee, right before we walked out on stage.

She looked genuinely puzzled. "No, are you?"

I shook my head, lying. I didn't want her to catch a case of my bundle of nerves.

But after we stepped out onstage and started "You Are My Sunshine," the feeling quickly changed. Mayzee's big voice ignited my energy, and I played my three-chord song like I'd never played it before. And Opa was right. The audience always knew when the performer was having a good time.

At the end of the evening, Opa invited all the performers back onstage, and we took requests. Some audience members had written theirs down earlier and dropped the notecards in her drummer's cowboy hat. Mayzee drew the first one, and Opa read it aloud: "I'm not sure I know this song. It says *squim. S-Q-U-I-M.* Anyone know that tune?"

Everyone laughed like it was a joke, but I knew what it meant. Somewhere out there in the audience was Twig, and she was saying she was sorry again.

Saturday, September 15
8:00 am - 6:00pm
All proceeds will go to
the new Antler Public Library

BURGESS AUCTION HOUSE

CHAPTER 42

Zachary Beaver went back to Florida the day after the opry show, but the buzz of his return still hadn't died down. Even Joe and I talked about him a lot. Which was a great distraction from what would be happening soon.

Joe was leaving in two days. We'd only been off for the summer a couple of weeks, but Mrs. Toscani wanted to get back to Brooklyn so that Joe would have a summer in the old neighborhood. They'd been excited to find a home down the street from their former one.

I was able to have some more time off because my parents had hired a new employee. He just needed to curb his enthusiasm about the Mustangs. Not every customer is a fan. Buster was starting out filling the cups of ice, but I had faith that he'd soon graduate to the syrups.

I hadn't planned how Joe and I would spend our last days together, but I started by riding over to see him and checking out the new paint job. When he came outside, he had a little friend at his heels.

I gave him a puzzled look.

"I know, I know, I said I didn't want a dog, but I couldn't stop thinking of him. I told Mom, and she thought he was just what I needed. Now I'll be taking a piece of Antler with me."

Mrs. Toscani opened the front door and waved at me. Then she called out, "Johnny Cash, time to eat!"

Johnny Cash raced back to the house.

"Looks like he's not just your dog."

We laughed and then we were quiet.

To break the silence, I almost told him how much better Miss Myrtie Mae's house looked painted blue.

Then I stopped myself. Instead I said, "Your home makes me think of the Panhandle sky after a storm, kind of a purplish-blue."

Joe grinned. "So it's finally *my* home? Now that I'm leaving in a couple of days."

"Well, the only reason I've been call—"

He softly tapped my shoulder with his fist. "I'm just kidding. The painter called it periwinkle, but it looks like purple to me."

A banner across the FOR SALE sign read TOO LATE, IT'S SOLD! Miss Earline was becoming an edgy marketer in her old age.

Mr. Pham, the new owner, had chosen the paint color. Mrs. Toscani was nice enough to let him start on his personal touches even though he hadn't officially closed yet. He was buying the house for his future fusion restaurant serving Vietnamese and American fare. Ferris said he reckoned the Bowl-a-Rama Café had been fusion and hadn't even known it. Mr. Pham's new restaurant was going to be fancy, though—white tablecloths and a dress code. The women could wear anything, but the men would have to wear a tie or cowboy boots.

Summer break had only just begun, but the sun beat down like it was July.

"I'm going to miss you," Joe said.

I kicked at my bike pedal causing it to spin.

"Don't you have a friend in New York?" he asked.

"Kate," I said. "Kate McKnight."

"Maybe you can visit her. Or maybe you can just come see us."

I liked the sound of that, our friendship continuing even though more than a thousand miles stretched between us. Long-distance friendships could happen. Dad, Uncle Cal, and Zachary were proof of it.

We were staring at the house when it seemed out of nowhere Twig rode up on her bike. Her hair blew about, having grown long enough to brush her shoulders.

"Hi," she said shyly. Then her tone took on its usual confidence. "The periwinkle shade with chalk colored trim is sharp. And so are the hot pink geraniums in the window boxes."

Together, Joe and I said, "Mr. Pham!"

He loved his flowers.

Twig wasn't done yet. "Those bronze gutters are classy. Why have plain gutters when you can have bronze?" Twig sure knew how to soak up every detail.

A second later, she asked, "Mr. Pham's idea?"

We nodded.

I took a closer look, trying to see something she may have missed.

Joe and I were quiet, so Twig spoke again. "I thought I might go see how the new library is coming along and then stop at Allsup's for a Dr Pepper. You two want to come?"

Joe and I exchanged glances, but we didn't say anything. Since this was one of our last days together, I'd hoped we were going to spend it alone. Maybe even check out Mrs. McKnight's rose tunnel.

Twig stared down at her sandals and fixed one foot on a pedal. She looked up with a plastered-on smile, and I knew she was hurt. "Well, see you around."

She pushed off.

Joe and I watched her ride away. I felt torn in half about what had happened to us since September. But she'd said she was sorry twice.

The wind stirred a tall patch of grass, and a tumble-weed rolled across the road, not stopping until it smacked into Joe's fence. Instead of collapsing, as expected, it stayed intact.

That's what we'd been since September—tumbleweeds—Joe, Twig, and me. Thinking we were so strong and independent, but we'd learned that we were fragile, too. Maybe we weren't made of sticks and debris, powered by the wind, but like tumbleweeds, we couldn't make it alone. We needed each other.

Twig was moving at a leisurely pace. She hadn't even made it halfway down the street.

Joe looked over at me, and it was as if we could read each other's thoughts. He hurried toward his porch and went after his bike while I hopped on mine. We pedaled fast, trying to catch up.

Twig didn't seem to know we were behind her, until I yelled, "Wait up!"

She slowed to a stop and glanced over her shoulder. The forced smile from a moment before was missing. In its place was the big one I knew by heart. Everything we'd done together since we were in second grade was wrapped up in it, trick-or-treating, Easter egg hunts, riding the back roads, and hanging at Allsup's. I wasn't sure where Twig and I would be next year or even five years from now, but today we needed to find out if anyone from Maine was making their way through Antler.

We Remember
9-11-01

CHAPTER 43

It's been a couple of months since Zachary's visit. Dad stays in touch with him, but not as much as Joe and I have with each other. My parents finally bought a computer, and most days I can count on an email from Joe, and he from me.

Joe says his mom is on the 9/11 memorial committee. They both have invited us to visit them in New York. Mom says maybe we can go next summer and make it our first official mother-daughter trip.

Every business in Antler has a collection jar for the memorial on their checkout counter, but our town also has its own monument of tribute. Mr. Pham donated the gazebo to the library, and it's now on the grounds with a plaque that reads WE REMEMBER, 9-11-01.

A copy of Zachary Beaver's book, *The Sideshow Kid*, is at the new library. Kennedy said the whole town must be on the wait list to read it. I'll always be thankful to Zachary, because in many ways, trying to find him opened the door to my friendship with Joe. Also the search would never have happened if it weren't for Miss Myrtie Mae and her love of photography. I look at the world differently because of her pictures, finding the extraordinary even in something as common as an empty bird feeder. Our gifts really do keep on giving.

Every Saturday I play at the opry, but I'm still trying to master those bar chords. Because of that, I haven't played "Sweet Afton" onstage yet. One day I will. When I do, it will be, as Twig and I used to say, *tob*.

Like the old times, Twig and I sometimes ride around town on our bikes. We include a stop at Mr. Pham's soon-to-open restaurant. I always look up at the window on the second floor and expect to see Joe sitting there or Miss Myrtie Mae peering out at the street from her first-floor bedroom.

Although we've mended our friendship, Twig and I haven't attempted another trip together back to the canyon overlook, but Dad and I have. He finally dragged his bike out of the shed. Since Joe left, we've been there a few times. Before heading out on the old back highway, we check the weather forecast. Dad says the road makes him think of Grandpa. They used to take it a lot when they were delivering worms. Which is probably why he points out landmarks we pass like Prairie Dog Town Fork even though he's done it many times before.

"Your grandfather loved this canyon," Dad tells me. "He said it was the reason he came to the Panhandle."

"Why didn't he move back to Dallas after Opa went away?" I ask, then wish I hadn't. We never talk about my grandparents' divorce.

Dad doesn't seem bothered by my question, even ponders it awhile, finally saying, "He was home."

We ride until we reach the twisted incline. Then we hide our bikes behind a mesquite and walk on the shoulder along the road up to the rim of the canyon. Making the climb leaves us breathless, but it's worth getting to the top.

Now I understand the magnetic pull of this place—it's rugged, yet open and hollow, as if God has carved out a big beautiful bowl from the earth. I always thought Twig wanted to ride here because she was rebellious, but I've changed my mind. This massive canyon cradles sorrows and lifts spirits.

Whenever I'm here, I close my eyes and imagine Joe standing on the rim, calling out to his dad. I visualize Uncle Cal too. And sometimes if the wind is blowing in just the right direction, I swear I can hear the names of all our loved ones who have passed, floating up to us and soaring on, not even stopping when they reach the clouds.

ACKNOWLEDGMENTS

Thank you, Jerry Holt, for reading several drafts of this story, finding typos, and questioning facts. He probably didn't know I would put him back to work after he retired. Thank you, Jerry, for your belief in my work and telling me twenty-six years ago to stop talking about writing and do it.

Shannon Holt, thanks for always giving me your honest feedback. Since you were seven you were my first reader. I'm not sure that's a fair thing for a mother to ask of her child, but know that I'm forever grateful.

I'm also grateful for Christy Ottaviano, who has always challenged me to dig deeper and reach for my best. Christy, working with you for the last twenty-four years has been one of the most rewarding experiences of my life. How did I get so lucky?

From the moment I met my agent, Amy Berkower, I knew she would be a good fit for me. It's rare to find a person with a keen sense of business mixed with warmth. Amy, you possess both. Thank you for fifteen years of guidance.

A special thank you to my friend and author, Lola

Schaefer, for being my accountability buddy as I wrote this story. It meant so much that you allowed me to check in daily.

As a reader I appreciate the details other writers put in their books. In my own work, those details often come from interviewing people and researching places. For this story, they are the following: musician Ray Miles, Billie from the Blanco Bowling Club Café, musician Seth Kessel, firefighters Vickie Hess-Miller and Ryan Miller, former ninepin-setter John Young, the 9/11 Memorial & Museum, Amarillo Public Library, Arlington Public Library. A special thank you to the *New York Times* journalists who covered the hours of the 9/11 tragedy and the days and months that followed. Their articles were an important source that helped me write about this time in our history.

The attacks of 9/11 were devastating to all American citizens, but the impact of that day became more real to me when a few months later Meredith Kennedy Andrews told me that her father, Robert C. Kennedy, "Bob," was one of the victims. She shared what Bob had meant to his family, and how that day had changed everything for them. Those conversations have stayed with me. I couldn't have written this book without Meredith. So I'm thankful to her and all the other survivors who continue to share their loved ones' stories with the world, forever reminding us of who we lost. May we never forget.